In the Empire of Dreams

Terence Gallagher

Published by Four Old Things Press, 2021.

Proofreading: Terence Gallagher and Kathleen Woodburn
Cover Design: Kathleen Woodburn
Cover Art, Copyright © Kathleen Woodburn

This is a work of fiction; any resemblance to persons living or dead is coincidental.

Chapter 1

THE MAN DESCENDED. It was a wooded slope, the trees well-spaced, tall, with dark trunks. The forest floor was soft and rolled under his feet as he walked. Little light threaded through the leaves. At the bottom, before he reached the river, the underbrush grew thick and he had to force his way through brambles. The popping and stretching startled birds, and they darted off into the shadow of the trees. At last he broke through, and stood above the bank of the river. There were no trees here.

The river was swift, not wide. Above the other bank the land rose in a cliff. The trees on the other bank were slender, short, bent, with small leaves; they fought for their place on the steep rock and rose at odd angles.

The man wore a hat with a long brim and a feather alongside. It shadowed his eyes and helped him see. He looked and he saw horsemen riding between the river and the cliff, along a path invisible to him. They rode fast. He could not make out their faces but he saw that there were five men riding with a woman, and he could see by the placement of her hands and by her carriage that they were taking her where she did not wish to go.

She rode a white horse and wore a long trailing blue gown. She turned toward him; she had seen him watching from the other bank. For a long moment they looked, those two, and then the horsemen passed from sight around the first bend of the winding river.

CONRAD LAY IN BED AND looked at the ceiling. Who was the man? he wondered. Was it me? Is it anyone?

He closed and opened his hands and stretched beneath the sheets, flexing his feet, wringing out his back, working his joints. Sometimes he awoke well before his alarm clock gave the signal and he would lie for a long time in bed staring up at the ceiling. He hoped that this was such a day, so he could consider at leisure what he had just seen.

The alarm rang.

When the alarm rang he had to rise. He could not afford to take chances with traffic on the way to work. He made time for breakfast, a boiled egg and English muffin, but not for coffee. He would get coffee at work. All through the winter, the road to Yonkers had been hard. If it wasn't snowing, the potholes slowed traffic, sometimes even breaking wheels and wrecking axles. Now, at the approach of spring, they would soon start filling the potholes at all hours of the day and night, and that would slow traffic in a new way.

His car was old but reliable, and he drove slowly along the ravaged Bronx River Parkway, avoiding the pits and pitfalls he had seen and noted on earlier trips. When he pulled into the lot, he parked in the space farthest from the door, as he always did, rain or shine. He still had a few minutes, so he sat with his hands on the wheel.

He squeezed and released the wheel a few times. He should get up early enough to exercise before he got to work, but he knew he wouldn't. He needed his sleep, all of it.

The others were arriving and it was time for him to start the day. It looked like anyplace, the place he worked. You couldn't tell what it was from the outside, or from the inside, at first. He stepped through the glass door and onto the same blue-carpeted floor he'd walked across for ten years. There were a few desks and half-height cubicles laid out immediately by the entrance. Conrad had been with the company long enough to rate an office of his own. It was small, but it had a window, and he had been happy to move in. Lately, though, it had begun to worry him, ever since they'd sent a man out from corporate headquarters, a finance man, a man of finances and financials, a clear and present danger. No one had ever explicitly stated this new man's role, but all the locals knew that it must be to save money by cutting waste.

The finance man's office was nearest the entrance, like a set trap, and Conrad had to walk past the open door coming and going. The dark destroyer, Sal Lagonigro by name, was at his desk early and late, surrounded by spreadsheets, by charts and printouts. He had a friendly word for everyone, Lagonigro, but just the one word, all the while working the whetstone, sharpening his knives.

Conrad knew these finance guys, he'd dealt with them before at other places in other lives. They had no understanding of the purposes of the institutions they dismantled, of the way the parts worked together to accomplish a design. They had one goal, to save money, and if they could demonstrate a savings, and a persuasive prediction of a future shift from red to black, they could flatter themselves on a job well done and move on, leaving others to deal with the wreckage. They thought they were realists, but they lived in a fantasy world of numbers without meaning.

On the other hand, Conrad had to admit that this Lagonigro had ample reason to cast an exacting eye on his own role with the company. Conrad was a tech guy, but a tech guy who was daily losing touch, his areas of expertise becoming more and more irrelevant. His role had devolved to the point that his main function was to be the wing man on product demonstrations, to make sure that the technology worked smoothly and to avoid embarrassing breaks before they occurred.

Conrad felt his worth melting away, a sensation almost physical, like the sand sliding from under his feet at the beach, when he used to stand in the foam in his childhood and let the action of the waves bury him up to the ankles.

There was a demo today. He and Bobby Kutta were going up to a private college to demonstrate the worth of their new online economics database. In the past they'd dealt only with businesses; this move into the field of education was a new one and seemed risky to Conrad. Nevertheless, he was ready when Bobby K came by his office. He had the projectors and screens packed and ready, with the extra lenses and bulbs.

Kutta drove them to the demo site. It would have been an embarrassment to the company for them to arrive in Conrad's old Toyota. Kutta leased an Audi with an excellent sound system, which he wasted on sports radio most of the time.

"You got your bracket ready?" he asked.

Conrad tried to follow sports enough to hold a conversation, but he drew the line at college basketball. Sixty-eight teams in the tournament and it seemed like a hundred out. That was too much like homework.

"Nah. I don't follow college basketball."

"Win some money. Gotta win some money." Bobby K was a go-getter. He went out there and made things happen, as he liked to say. Conrad was grateful for the radio, which made what would have been a difficult conversation unnecessary and required only easy reaction, to the radio and to Bobby K's comments.

Demos interested Conrad chiefly for the chance to meet new people. The academic demonstrations afforded a new registry of humanity for Conrad to observe. They met in a big classroom, a sort of lecture hall with a dais, in the oldest building on campus. There was a paucity of outlets, but the setup was easy, because Conrad had brought extension cords, though they were severely discouraged in the manual.

As he set up, he took stock of the assembly. The persons of chief interest were a fetching middle-aged woman with auburn hair, wrapped up in an artistically-draped paisley neck scarf, and a know-it-all.

The know-it-all did most of the talking.

"What is that, a screen?" he giggled. "We have a fully interactive smartboard you can use."

This guy was probably an administrator or department head. Conrad had found that these petty potentates often liked to maintain and flaunt a knowledge of the latest technology in their field. In fact, Conrad had been told the man's name and position as soon as they'd met, but promptly forgot it. The auburn woman's name was Carolyn Eames.

Kutta explained that they didn't need internet connectivity because their demonstration was "canned"–he didn't use that word–rather than live. It was basically a series of screen shots. Even for an academic audience that was not inspiring. As Kutta said later in the car, "That's gonna have to change." Conrad agreed, though he knew that the change would move him one step closer to the door.

Kutta was an old pro and he managed to dispel the initial bad impression with a lot of technical vocabulary, couched at just the right level of complexity so the know-it-all could flatter himself that he understood it. Kutta made him an ally and he helped explain difficult concepts to his colleagues. They talked a lot about data points, the sheer number of data points that went into this mighty database. Conrad wondered how many data points were of any actual use or significance. Or were they just assembled and counted to hit an arbitrary figure, the way libraries used to do with books to meet accreditation standards?

Conrad kept everything humming along seamlessly. The auburn lady was a political science professor. She asked a couple of questions but none that fell under Conrad's purview. She was shrewd and she easily divined, despite Kutta's best efforts, that the product would be of no use to her or her department. She wore a trim short navy jacket and a plaid pleated skirt and heels that were really quite sassy for a woman of her age. Conrad was looking forward to the promised coffee and cake afterwards, when he would endeavor to engage her in conversation and to experience her atmosphere and test her aura. He had hopes that some connection could be made.

When the time came, however, she announced that she had a class to give, and after a gracious goodbye, she clap-clicked smartly out of the room, taking her hair, her scarf, her skirt, and those shoes away forever. Isn't that always the way? Conrad thought. He drowned his disappointment in coffee.

On the way back to the office, Kutta and Conrad discussed the demonstration. Kutta was genuinely interested in what Conrad had to say. They were as different as night and day, but Kutta understood that Conrad's very oddity meant that he might possess knowledge and insights that he himself did not.

"Think they'll go for it?"

"I don't know. The main guy, the talker, seemed to go for it. The others, it's hard to tell. The Polisci prof, Carolyn, was unamused. But I think they perked up when they heard the introductory offer."

"I had to fight to put that in. We lose money the first two years."

"It's worth it. Once a college picks it up, they're likely to keep it through sheer inertia."

"That's what I thought. You got to think long-term. But you try to tell that to the budget office."

Conrad nodded.

"I think they'll go for it," he said at last.

"So do I. So do I."

They arrived back at the office in the mid-afternoon. Kutta, who had been a reasonable companion during the demonstration and on the car ride home, shifted back into Bobby K, peppering his colleagues with meaningless raillery: "Daniel, looking sharp, does the boss know you stole his tie?"; "Maia, Greece is going down tonight ... the qualifiers, Greece is taking a fall." Conrad had no idea if people actively liked Bobby K, tolerated him, or despised him, and he wondered if Bobby K had any idea himself.

Conrad methodically put his paraphernalia away, first checking each item for damage or wear. The less he had to do, the more careful he was doing it. The common practice after these demos was for Conrad and Kutta to meet with the boss as soon as they got settled, and to give him a sense of how well the demonstration had gone and what would likely be their best follow-up strategy. Today, however, the boss was closeted in a meeting, so Conrad had some time on his hands.

He stood in the doorway, looking over the office floor. It was the usual scene as the clock swept through its slow progress toward quitting time. Someone was hovering around Lydia's desk. Lydia was the new personal assistant to the boss, an olive-skinned, quiet, somewhat mysterious young lady. She didn't speak much, and was so new that Conrad hadn't yet figured out her accent. Otherwise, there were people crossing the floor with papers in their hands, taking care of the routine office tasks that they liked to leave for the end of the day. Conrad heard the distant sound of a copier door being rammed shut, primed with another load of paper that would shortly be spit out and shortly after that thrown away.

He knew all these people by name, some he had worked with for years, but no one here was a friend. They were reasonably friendly, work-friendly, but not friends. So what was it, this business here, this life? Suppose he wasn't fired for general uselessness, suppose he played out the string day after day till retirement? Thirty or forty years absorbed in elaborate pointlessness, a strange game constructed by person or persons unknown to keep the animals busy. Half these people, when they retired they looked for part-time work or they volunteered somewhere, because "they didn't know what to do with themselves." Animals accustomed to their cages.

Why all this bother about life, this anguish and conflict, who lives, who dies, how long, people willing to fight and struggle and suffer for something that was of so little use to them? Those who had families, that was something, whatever temporary configuration their families happened to take, they could draw meaning from that, they could devote their lives to their families or tell themselves that they were doing so. But what was that but vain repetition? They agonized over their children, over what school they got into, over their extracurriculars and internships, and at the end of it all their children issued forth into exactly the same meaningless lives as their parents had endured. Strange, it all seemed strange to Conrad.

Kutta came by Conrad's office and told him that the Boss was still locked in "a steel-cage death match" with Lagonigro. They would have to meet tomorrow. That was short-term good, since a meeting avoided was always a good thing, and long-term bad, since anything the two of them cooked up in secret was likely to cause trouble for everyone else. After Kutta left, Conrad stood in his doorway for a minute or so and watched the world go by, his tiny, odd, insipid little slice of the world. Then he sat back down at his desk to contemplate the mystery.

CONRAD ATE ALONE OFF fine china. His house was cool and dark and dusty. He had inherited it when his parents died, first his father then his mother within the year. He could sell it and make a million, such was the madness of the New York housing market. He could sell out and move far away. But when he tried to think of where he might move, his imaginings grew hazy and unmoored to reality and he conjured up places that were movie sets or story openings, places that didn't exist.

His house was his country. This is my own my native land. His memories, and the memories of his people, were on the walls and in the bookshelves. He spun the music of his ancestors on the old family turntable. Outside was confusion and oppression and the desire to dominate and destroy him. Every night when he pulled into the driveway he was returning to a fort. To leave it was surrender and exile.

So he sat and drank wine at the head of an empty table. Perhaps he would dream again tonight.

THE MAN SAT IN THE corner and dipped torn pieces of bread into stew. He was tucked into a nook made by a bending staircase that rose behind him. He ate slowly and watched the bar. People kept coming in off the ferry. At the man's small round table there was only a woman in dark clothes, feeding a fat little dazed boy, putting tidbits in his mouth like a bird. At length three men entered the tavern wearing black livery. They spoke loudly to one another and when they approached the bar, those already drinking shrank away to create space. The man recognized their uniforms—he had seen men so dressed bringing the woman in blue along the river. He spoke to his table companion, calling her attention to the new arrivals.

"Those men in the black surcoats. Who are they?"

She shook her head and looked down. He did not ask again.

He waited until the barmaid came again to his table, with a puffing stein. A fresh, sweating girl, could she even be sixteen?

"Those men, *schatz*. Those three men in black close to the door. Who are they? What is that livery?"

The girl gave him a quick fearful look, but answered, too young to be cautious.

"They are *Die Bruderschaft. Die Bruderschaft des Rabe.*"

"Whom do they serve?"

"I think they serve no one."

She hurried away.

The Brotherhood of the Raven. The man sat and stroked his chin and watched the strangers drink.

WHEN CONRAD AWOKE, the first thought that occurred to him was, "so the man is over the river." He didn't know how he'd gotten across, but he was sure that the tavern stood by the water under the beetling cliffs.

It was early, just six o'clock. He decided to rise and make himself a big breakfast. These dreams made him hungry. They reminded him of his trip to Europe, five years ago now, after his parents' death, when he visited for the first time since childhood the land of his grandfather. Every morning there would be a sumptuous breakfast at his hotel: eggs, bacon, sausages, many kinds of bread, creamy running yogurt with berries straight from the farm. Since he'd come back to New York, he'd gotten used again to a quick boiled egg and a slice of toast or bowl of cereal.

Today he tried to recreate the comfort, the joy, of a really good breakfast. He came close, used up all his remaining eggs, but by the time he'd cleaned up he was almost-late. For once, the traffic broke his way and he pulled into his parking space just at eight thirty.

Lydia was at her post.

"Mr. Noakes wants to meet with you and Bobby K at nine. He asked me to tell you."

Look at the way she arranged her little station. Pictures, stacks of colored Post-its, laminated charts and contact sheets fixed to the grey walls. A dark green leafy plant by her feet in a fancy glazed pot. God bless her. She was still new to the world of work, Conrad thought, still young enough to be excited by it. Onward and upward. Like the auburn woman of yesterday, she wore a scarf in what Conrad believed to be a French twist. That must be a style.

In his office, Conrad looked through the morning's emails and then gathered his few notes from yesterday's demo. If Noakes is meeting with us both, he thought, it probably doesn't have anything to do with the long budget meeting with Lagonigro yesterday. So no layoffs today? He watched the wall clock move slowly toward nine and thought about scrambled eggs.

At nine precisely he was standing in front of the boss's front door.

He saw Lydia on her island, with the receiver in her hand.

"I was just going to call you. You can walk right in."

When Conrad rapped smartly and entered he saw Kutta already sitting in the office. Had they started before him? They had. Did he care? Not as much as he should.

As he settled into his seat, the Boss asked, "So what did you think?"

Conrad gave him a quick summation of the demo, and when he finished the Boss said, "That's pretty much what Bobby said." Then added: "So. We'll chalk that up as a probable."

"It depends if there are further layers of decision-makers. But I think the people in the room went for it."

"OK, the other thing we need to talk about is the nature of the demos themselves. Bobby tells me the canned demos aren't cutting it anymore and he says you agree."

"Well, they're perfectly adequate to demonstrate the product. But people expect more now. And I guess that's what counts."

"That's what counts. So, what are we going to do about it?"

Conrad could see they had already decided what to do about it.

They talked about it for a while. The new demo would be based off the current academic subscription, but simplified.

"We've got to keep it simple so things don't fall apart in the middle of a demonstration," said Kutta.

"Don't you trust your product?" asked the Boss.

"I trust my product. I don't trust my customers."

Conrad was to take the lead in developing the new demo. It was beyond him, technically and probably by now conceptually, and everyone in the room knew it.

When it was time to get up to leave, he made a final effort.

"We should keep the canned demo, though. Not everyone is going to have the setup for a live one."

Yes, sure, they agreed they should "keep" the old demo. Somewhere in a closet, no doubt.

It didn't matter. It was time for a change, Conrad thought. High time for a change.

CONRAD WAS DISAPPOINTED in himself. He thought that he'd accepted his coming change of life with equanimity, but when the word was finally spoken he must have become more agitated than he'd realized. The traffic was bad coming home, his mind was wandering in new paths, and he actually took the wrong exit from the expressway, one exit before his usual. It was not a serious inconvenience, as the exits were less than a mile apart, but it was an embarrassment. He decided to make a virtue out of an error, and turned off toward the Park, down by the salt water, that had been his local park since he was a boy. It was supposed to close at dusk, but he was not surprised to see that the parking lot was still open, though the sun had long ago gone down in the west.

He parked beneath the lights. He had thought to sit on a bench, but that now he was here he found that this held no appeal. He left the path and walked under the trees, forcing himself through the underbrush when it grew thick, holding his elbows high to protect his eyes. At length he reached the edge of the park, where a high bluff overlooked a crowded parkway and beyond it a small bay and beyond that the scattered Christmas-tree lights of a hundred houses on the opposite shore. When he was a boy he sometimes likened the rushing sound of the parkway cars to surf and pretended he was on the shore of a great ocean.

Not today. The rush-hour traffic was packed in both directions. He sat on the splintered stump of a blasted tree and watched the cars in their painful progress below him, white lights turning to red one after the other as they passed. He knew there was a full bottle of Riesling in the refrigerator at home, bottled in Rüdesheim, and breaded cutlets left over from the weekend. He watched and pitied the creeping slaves below him.

It was passing away. It would end soon. He was too young to retire, too old to find a new job without marketable skills. He'd worked the same job for many years yet still he had no skills. That's what happens when you work in a line that's not suited for you. You don't keep up. The work is noxious enough, but to spend the extra hours in training, taking classes, reading journals. It was impossible. He had not enough money saved to retire. He would have to sell.

He sat for a long time, enjoying the view, enjoying the air. He looked up at the night sky, at the stars through the branches. Time to go home.

As he stepped back into the light, approaching the lot through tall grass, he heard a sound he had not heard for a long long time. The sound of an empty bottle sent skittering over the concrete, sent by a kick. He was just in time to see a brown beer bottle rolling past the back of his car, finishing its journey.

His was the only car in the lot now. To the left, at the corner of the lot, some sitting, some standing, a small group of men was gathered, drinking beer and talking loudly. They noticed him and their voices dropped to a conspiratorial tone. It was a scene from his youth, from the seventies, when broken glass over concrete was a common sight. He opened his car door, but before he entered, he stepped back and took a quick look beneath the chassis and behind the wheels.

Someone called to him.

He had no interest in these men.

He backed the car off in one long motion, only starting the J-turn when he was near the exit.

"Hey! Yo!"

More seventies stuff. Someone threw a bottle. It only reached half-way to the car and spilled liquid when it struck ground, which offended Conrad by the waste.

The exit was locked. The barred iron gate was pulled to and chained. Someone from the Parks Department must have closed up during his reverie. This was no matter. There were many exits from the park and Conrad knew them all. It was *his* park.

He turned left and bumped over the curb. Some of the men had begun running towards him, in what looked like a mock charge. He cruised along the foot path in front of the tennis courts, trying to go slowly enough to entice them to continue chasing. They kept at it for a while; he watched them in the rear view mirror. When he got under the high trees they gave up. Too bad; he had to make a sharp right before the playground and they could have caught him if they'd cut diagonally over the grass. He emerged from a path marked "authorized vehicles only" and rejoined the city streets.

Chapter 2

THE FIRST SOUND WAS horses snorting.

The man turned and looked behind him. He was walking along the riverside, in a gravelly place where the cliffs drew back from the bank. Behind him the rock face pinched close to the water. He had just come through that narrow place but he had not noticed the three horsemen sheltering on the near side of the rocks.

They came out at a walk and occupied the path behind him. The man was on foot. The horsemen were armed with lances and wore the livery of the Brotherhood of the Raven. They must have heard him talking at the tavern, asking about them. Or perhaps some spy had informed.

They spoke no word. One urged his horse forward, and then to a trot, and then set his spurs to the animal's side.

The man jumped from the path, scrambling, dropping down to the tumbled rocks by the water. His feet were in the river. He drew his sword. Let them try to bring their horses down here.

The three horsemen gathered above him, then dismounted. Two came down over the rocks with swords drawn, while one stayed on the path, still holding his spear.

The man picked his way along the river rocks, moving back towards the bottleneck. Perhaps in their pursuit they would become separated and he could deal with them individually.

They were wise. They kept together. Already he was parrying thrusts. It was a matter of time before he lost his footing or the man on the path threw his spear.

"Gentlemen, gentlemen."

A new player, a man seated at his ease on a big boulder up along the path, watching the contest.

"Three set against one. It is not a pretty thing."

"Mind your business," said the spearman on the path. "Don't meddle with the Brotherhood if you know what's good for you."

"Affairs of the sword are always my business," the new man said. "And I have never known what was good for me. And so ..."

And he flung himself at the spearman, so quick that the man had to drop his spear and step back just for room to draw his sword.

The man in the river took his opportunity. Both of his foemen had turned their heads to look at the new player. A long lunge, just as they turned back to look at him, and the foremost of his enemies lay dying from a wound in the throat. The other leapt upon him in wrath, and the two fought long in the water.

Their footwork was constrained and they wound up grappling hilt to hilt. The man dragged his foeman to a place in the river where he had already stepped and he knew there was a pothole. When the other stepped in and lost his footing, the man spun him round and pushed him on his back in the water. Before the other could rise, the man had let go the double-grip on his sword, snatched out his dagger and dispatched his opponent. He watched him sink in the river, then cleaned his dagger in the water and wiped it on his shirt as he climbed up to the path. Just before he reached the top, a hand reached down and helped pull him to the top.

"That was well done," said a voice.

The man looked at his deliverer. He saw a smooth-shaven face, an older face than he would have thought from the ringing, merry voice. A long nose, cut across the bridge by a scar that ran into the left eyebrow. Dark, watchful eyes. Dark clothes, stained and worn by long use and travel, but accented here and there with gold braid, gold buttons, and white cuffs. Across the dark padded front, like a velvet breastplate, a single golden device in the shape of a lightning bolt.

It was Flik-Flak!

WHO THE HELL IS FLIK-Flak? Conrad asked himself. The alarm shocked him awake. He kept the clock on his dresser, and when he rolled out of bed to rise and stop the ringing, he found his leg was asleep. He fell to the floor and had to crawl across the boards to reach his dresser. He could not help but laugh.

When silence was restored, he sat at the edge of his bed and massaged his leg back to life. Flik-Flak. Who is Flik-Flak? In the dream I knew him. In the dream everybody knew him.

Conrad had finished the bottle of Dragonstone the night before. Riesling is an easy wine. It made for a pleasant night and a pleasant dream. He felt fine when he arose, physically alert, on point, but he was conscious of an overwhelming reluctance to go to work. Now that he was sure that the end was coming very soon, it seemed pointless to consume more of his days with this nonsense.

Make a game of it. Play out your hand. Force them to make the last move.

But all those lost days. Well, he made up for them at night.

THINGS STARTED CHANGING at work. The boss was unavailable more and more often, behind a shut door or out of the office, even out of the state. In his absence, Lydia became an indispensable conduit.

"He'll be in meetings all day."

"I don't know if I'm supposed to send this out or if he wants to look at it again."

"Is that the Spec Sheet?"

"Yes."

"He said to hold on to it until he gets back. There may have to be some changes."

Could this be the start of a meteoric rise?

The old familiar faces started vanishing from their cubicles without comment, cake, or sendoff. Sometimes they were replaced by temps. More often, not.

For his part, Conrad received an administrator's account to the academic database, Econstar Academy, and several thick binders of documentation. He requested and received access to the demonstration modules of other company databases, to compare and contrast, and to copy in his attempts to create the new Academy demonstration. He faced this wonderland of permissions and gateways and sheer information without any clear idea of where to go next. He had a meeting scheduled next week with a serious tech person. It would be a nice calculation how much he could lean on this fellow without it becoming obvious that he was completely out of his depth.

On his way to work one day, it happened that a car somewhere along the road had wrecked a wheel in a pothole in the right lane, while another car, a little further along, had clipped the divider and come to rest in the left lane. With all the rush-hour traffic filing through a single lane, the parkway came almost to a complete stop. Conrad did not yet know the cause of the delay, though he could guess the general outlines, but he accepted the enforced stoppage as an occasion for rest and quiet reflection.

Parked as he was on the parkway, Conrad took the opportunity to examine the road's surface. He was amazed how bad its condition was. He knew, rattling over the ravaged concrete at fifty-five miles an hour, that there were some irregularities and holes. But he was looking at craters, some so deep that he could see the original metal grill underlying the road. It was a miracle that any car made it past this gauntlet.

He looked over at the saplings and brambles by the side of the road, still bare from winter, running up a slope to the city streets above.

He could see the lower part of some apartment buildings, facing the parkway across what must be the service road.

He stared, his idle curiosity suddenly forced to rigid attention. He could see a white horse–a steed–climbing through the foliage just at the top of the slope and then turning into the bare street. He could not get a view of the rider, but the horse was clear. A policeman? But he'd never seen a mounted policeman riding through rough terrain, and policemen do not ride white horses. He leaned across the gear shift into the passenger seat in an effort to see out from under the car roof and follow the horse's progress. He leaned; he stretched; he stared.

A crying angry horn brought him back to his situation. The traffic was moving again. Had he dozed off? He started forward, slowly. There was an exit only a few hundred feet down the road and he thought for a moment to turn off and find the white horse. But habit prevailed and he drove onward.

Could it be the woman in blue? But how did she get away from the Brotherhood?

He pondered these things.

At work Conrad lost almost the whole day because the IT department had begun its periodic maintenance on the Econstar database, which affected all the work he'd been doing. If they'd told him ahead of time, he could have provided against the damage, but they did not see fit to do that. Or they simply forgot. Aside from dropping them a pointed email, Conrad did not complain, certainly not to the boss like a child to its teacher. All his life he had scorned to do such; all his life he had suffered for it.

"WHY DOES THE BLACK Brotherhood have such an interest in you?"

"I don't really know."

"My friend ..."

"It's true. I can guess, though."

"So ..."

"In the tavern by the river, I was asking about them. They must have heard. And I had a reason to ask. I saw the Brotherhood, five or six of them, bringing a captive woman along the banks of the river. I wanted to know where they were going."

"You know this woman?"

"I only saw her the once. From across the river."

"Ah, but that is very romantic," said Peregrina. She came over to sit by Flik-Flak. She was tall, with a great mass of auburn hair, and wore a long leather dress and neat black boots with high square heels. "We must help this man find his lost lady."

They were in Flik-Flak's lair, an abandoned castle up in the hills, where Flik-Flak was living with his men and with the famous Peregrina. They had a fire going against the night and the open roof, and they were passing a bottle of Portuguese wine back and forth across the table.

After a pause, Flik-Flak spoke.

"It so happens, I know something about this situation."

"You know where she is?"

"I know where they were taking her. It is my practice to keep apprised of the movements of the Brotherhood when they pass close to my lands. We are not friends, the Brotherhood and I. So ... The woman is the Contessa, that is Gräfin, of Mittelsbach. She is being taken to the Castle Reichenstein to marry the Baron."

Peregrina clapped her hands. "Oh. It is she."

"I don't think the marriage pleases her. Even across the river I could see that."

"It is not a marriage of love or passion, I assure you. The Gräfin's father recently died and she has come into a very interesting inheritance. It is this inheritance that attracts Reichenstein's Baron. I know this man," he added thoughtfully. "A man of iron and smoke. A man to be feared, if one were anyone other than Flik-Flak. Or, perhaps, his new friend ..." and he lifted a glass.

"If your new friend had Flik-Flak by his side ... who knows?"

"Yes, yes," said Peregrina. "This marriage cannot be agreeable to the Countess. We must rescue her. Let us make a pledge."

THE RUMORS HAD STARTED at work.

"Did you hear? We're moving to Texas."

"I'm not going to Texas."

Conrad was sitting in the break room eating lunch from spread tinfoil, listening to the others. He did not believe that the office was moving to Texas–and he was *sure* they would not take him to Texas–but it interested him to listen.

"What makes you think we're moving to Texas?" An old hand, a skeptic.

"I was talking to someone at corporate. I won't name names. They are looking at real estate in Austin. They're heavy into real estate in Austin."

"So, maybe corporate is moving. Or they're opening another branch."

"We're not opening any more branches, believe me."

"I'm not moving to Texas."

"What's wrong with Texas?" Kutta was stopping by the vending machine to stoke up on energy drinks. "No state income tax."

"Yeah, well it ain't New York."

"You'll love it."

Conrad could see that Kutta had no inside information and it was eating at him.

Lydia floated in. She brought a home-made salad. She did not buy a drink; she had brought bottled water from home. Conversation flagged for a short time, then someone asked her point blank.

"So what about this Texas move? Have you heard anything?"

"Sorry what?"

"The rumor is, we're moving to Texas. Have you heard anything?"

Lydia gave a sphinxlike smile and shook her head.

"No. I hope not. I just got a new apartment."

Some of these people had been here five, ten, fifteen years longer than Lydia but they all looked to her for news. It was impossible to believe that she did not know more than she was admitting.

So young and already so mysterious. Conrad watched her with admiration as she picked through her salad. The half-smile, the straight rudder-like nose, the little bright eyes, the satin skin, tan by nature not by sun. Romanian? Bulgarian? He could always ask her, but that would not be not sporting.

"Why don't you ask Lagonigro?" asked Kutta.

"Why don't you?"

"Hey, I'm not the one who's obsessing."

To Conrad it was like watching a Thursday night football game between two out-of-town teams. No skin in the game, as they say, but it passed the time.

WHEN CONRAD GOT HOME, before he ate dinner, he climbed up to the third floor. He rarely came up here, using the space mainly for storage of his parents' old effects. He sat in the front room and looked down on the street, on the late-returning workers walking to their cars.

As a boy, he liked to visit his mother in this front attic room. She used to paint up here during the temperate months, before the summer sun made it unbearable. (She hated air conditioning and wouldn't install it.)

Whenever Conrad came up, his mother would set down her pallet and brushes. After he saw and admired her latest work, they would sit at the front window to watch the world. When he was very young he would sit on her lap; when he got older he knelt at the window beside her chair. There were many levels. The householders puttering about their lawns. The commuters going to ground inside their cars. The squirrels dancing along the wires. The sparrows hopping and chirping in the branches. And far away, over the houses, the soaring birds, gulls and, on a lucky day, geese. All was theirs, all was theirs, sitting in the "tower room."

Conrad sat alone on his mother's little spindle chair until it got dark. There were no working bulbs in the room and when he finally got up to leave, he almost fell over a box loaded with her old painting supplies. All this would have to go when he moved. All this would be thrown away.

PEREGRINA SPUN HIM toward the door. A tall, well-built woman with a sturdy strong back and fragrant hair. She wore a mask. They all wore masks.

"Now," she said. "Now is the time. Through this door you will find the corridor to the south tower. Liese will guide you."

She spun back to the dance.

The man paused at the door and looked back at the room. They were in the banquet hall of Castle Reichenstein, attending a *ballo en maschera*. The room was all in a whirl, as the dancers turned and whooped, wilder and wilder as the night progressed. The man thought there was some madness on them that would only grow keener with time. It was Peregrina who had opened the way to the castle, Peregrina who had claimed an invitation, Peregrina who was desired and admired in all the dark and dangerous corners of the world.

The Baron did not dance. He was seated at the high table, watching the spectacle. The man had felt the Baron's eyes following him and wondered if he harbored suspicions of this unheralded stranger. Possibly ... probably ... he had only been watching the man's partner,

Peregrina. The Baron was attended now on either side by silk-clad lovelies, despite his planned wedding to the woman in the south tower. He paid them little mind, only twirled his wine stem and watched the dancers.

The fiddles sawed. The partners spun and clapped. The man stepped away, out through the open door.

He hurried along the corridor, in the direction Peregrina had given. The floor slanted downwards, then over two descending steps, then slanted down again, and to the left.

At a crossing hall, there was Liese waiting, a tiny neat nervous girl with a mass of pure yellow hair, in a neat serving woman's dress overlaid with a white apron.

"Come," she said, and led him away swiftly. Once or twice they passed other guests paired up or single men with their own captured serving wenches, wandering the halls looking for a private place to take their sport. But Liese led him further away down dim alleys, holding his hand in her little soft damp palm. The castle was built to confuse enemies and interlopers and soon the man too was bewildered.

She stopped before a dark arched doorway, at the landing of a tight spiral staircase that rose into blackness.

Liese dropped his hand and fished in her apron pocket.

"Here is the key to the lady's room. When you bring her down you must lock the door behind you and take the key with you. It is a copy secretly made. I will wait for you. You must take me with you when you go. If I remain here I will be killed. The Baron will know I betrayed him. Hurry!" and she handed him her guiding lantern.

The man climbed the narrow stairs on shaky legs. At the top, he laid the lantern on the broad part of the second step, and leaned against the close curved wall as he jiggle-fit the key in the lock. Once in, it turned easily.

The door swung without a noise. He had to duck to fit through the doorway. He stepped into a round white-painted tower room, brightly lit, with a cheerful fire in the hearth. Opposite the door and near the fire lay a richly caparisoned canopy bed and on the bed sat the lady.

She had been reading and had just laid the book down when she heard the key in the door. Her legs were swung over the side of the bed, as if she was ready to rise, and her body turned at the waist to face the door and whatever would come through.

"Who are you?" she asked. "What do you want? And why are you wearing that mask?"

He quickly took the mask from his face.

"I am Conrad. I am come to take you away from here if you are willing to go."

"I recognize you. The man across the river. Then you are real."

OVER THE NEXT FEW WEEKS, it became a regular occurrence for Conrad to meet with the "serious tech person." The person, Daniel Herrick by name, was serious in many senses of the word. Serious in demeanor, serious about technology and his job, and, strangest of all, serious about helping Conrad. Rare among his tribe, he was always ready to back up and explain again, on those frequent occasions when Conrad missed a step, or misunderstood a concept.

Conrad was intrigued by Herrick's mournful demeanor. He thought it was habitual, not a result of dissatisfaction at his role as tutor. Conrad had met doctors like that, sad-eyed, soft-spoken types, perhaps more comfortable with the raw exercise of their expertise than with the customer service interaction that perforce went with it. There was something more with Herrick. Was he dissatisfied with his life? Wished he'd chosen a different path? More than once, when Conrad looked up from pecking at the keys and peering at the screen with his face six inches away from the glow, he saw Herrick staring fixedly not to say wistfully out the window. Another dreamer perhaps? How many of us are there?

He found himself growing friendly towards this melancholy tech person.

In the late afternoon, at the end of a session, Herrick took off his glasses, sat back and ran his hands through his hair.

"Well I think that's as far as we can go with what we've got. At this point, the thing to do is start testing. See how it works in a simulation. That's the only way you'll be able to see what works and what doesn't work for the actual customers."

"We'll get Kutta involved in that. He's the one who's gonna be using it."

"Bobby K?"
Conrad smiled.
"I know. He's good though, very sharp when it comes to his job."
"Oh, I'm sure, I didn't mean ..."
"I know."
They both smiled.

"After he gets a look at it, we'll need to try it with an audience. We should recruit some people who aren't involved in product development or sales."

Lydia, thought Conrad. We'll definitely get Lydia involved in that.

THAT NIGHT, DRIVING home in the dark, Conrad chanced to look across the road at the place of the white horse and he saw figures climbing the slope through the underbrush. Only a moment and then he was gone, driving with the traffic towards the south. The figures seemed to be in city uniforms of some kind, as if they were Parks Department workers or Department of Transportation workers. Conrad doubted them. The Brotherhood? But what were they doing here? Who were they after? He contemplated these and other questions as he navigated the crowded highway and at length approached the homeward bridge, a suspended string of festive lights crossing the dark water in a graceful double sweep. Its beauty never failed to move him.

There was safety over the water, he thought. Safety at home.

Chapter 3

HURRYING AWAY, HURRYING from the door. There was some trouble behind, Conrad was sure of it. First blood had been drawn. They left by a little gate, a wooden door at the base of the tower, and Conrad's sword was clear of the sheath and in his hand. Others were with him, two women, a little and a big.

He remembered.

They'd broken out of Baron Reichenstein's castle and he was with the Contessa and little Liese, rescuing the Contessa. He heard voices, close behind them. A horn blew a long urgent note from the walls. The women wore dresses, the Contessa a long night dress, and they were on foot. They would all be caught. Was there a plan?

They were at the base of the castle wall now. They'd followed a gradual curving path and were standing in a wide flat space of dirt and gravel well packed by traffic, foot and horse. Conrad could see the main gate lowering and could hear the great chains rattle.

"Here, here."

Peregrina was waiting, seated on one horse and holding another by the bridle. There *was* a plan.

"Conrad, up on the black. Contessa with me. Hurry."

Conrad helped the Countess, encumbered by her heavy clothing, up behind Peregrina. He mounted the other horse, then reached down and hauled Liese, no great weight, up behind him as she struggled to help. The horses, caught up in their riders' excitement, sidestepped, turned and tossed their heads.

"Follow me close! Flik-Flak has our escape prepared along the river."

Not a moment too soon. The Baron's footmen were already running across the drawbridge and Conrad expected at any moment to hear the clatter of hooves on wood.

"Away!"

Peregrina set her boots to her horse and rode at a great pace, her hair streaming behind like a red-brown banner.

As soon as they passed beyond the lights of the castle, night closed around them. It was all Conrad could do to keep up on the unfamiliar paths. Liese was no horsewoman and she clung to Conrad's waist, trying unsuccessfully to suppress a long-drawn-out whimper of fear. Conrad laid a reassuring hand on hers, which calmed her but made the horse harder to manage. As they rode on, he began to see that he could trust his mount—even in the dark it could follow its companion.

They followed at first an upward path through the trees, which perplexed Conrad as he was expecting a straight run to the river. But they kept rising and he saw that they were going to go up the rocky slope and clear over the ridge. As the footing got tricky they slowed to a purposeful walk. At the top, with the speckled sky above them and the river gleaming below, they stopped for breath. They were standing at the foot of a ruined tower. Conrad looked back and saw the Baron's castle behind them on a less lofty summit. Then it was forward again. The river was ahead now, and Conrad saw that they had cut across one of the river's many bends and were descending again to the water's edge.

The horses went slower on the way down, following a path with many switchbacks. Conrad listened hard for the pursuit, but under the sounds of wind and water he could discern little. On the way up he had heard two or three times horns blowing, but now even that sound was gone.

As they came toward the river, the trees thickened and the slope grew more gradual. They reached the path at the base of the cliff, and Peregrina pulled her steed's head right and quickened its pace to a canter. It wasn't long before she stopped, and here was Flik-Flak in the path, smoking and waiting.

"Well performed," he said. "Admirable. Now you must dismount and follow me to the river."

They slid, jumped, or were lifted off the horses, and followed him down the rocks, single file.

Conrad heard Liese, "Ooh, where is he going? Why are we going to the river?"

They got to a broad flat landing place and saw a river boat, an odd sort of raft with gunwales and a high prow, bobbing in the black shallow water. There were two men waiting before them, leaning on poles, ready to push off.

"Come, come," said Flik-Flak. "They will not follow us here."

"Oh, no, I am afraid of the river," said Liese. "And at night! Who can navigate the river at night?"

"Fear not," said Peregrina. "Flik-Flak knows the river. We will come to no harm."

Liese and the Contessa were bundled onto the boat.

"Go up and drive those horses away," said Flik-Flak, for the horses were lingering where they had been left, waiting for their riders' return. "If the Baron's men see them waiting there they will know we left by water."

Peregrina and Conrad huffed up the rocks.

"That boat is too small," Peregrina muttered. "We'll sit too low. The little Liese was right to worry."

They struggled up to the flat path, when suddenly Peregrina whirled around.

"What are you doing?" Conrad heard her cry, and he too looked down at the river.

The river raft had detached from the bank and was floating down the current, with Flik-Flak's henchmen working the long poles like oars. Liese gave a great wail of fear.

Flik-Flak addressed them.

"Dearest lady, it does me great distress to leave you like this, and you too, my new-made friend. But alas my plans are such that there is no place for you with me at this time.

"You swine," Peregrina raged on the bank. "Betrayer! Do you think I will not find you? Do you think I will not come upon you in the end?"

"It will always be a joy to see you, dear lady. But I think I should warn you that when you see me again, it is my hope and intention to be a married man. And for now," he made an elaborate flourish, "hail and farewell."

The boat disappeared into darkness.

"That swine. That ogre. He will pay. Always boasting of his treacheries and he dares to practice them on me."

"On us."

"On us, of course. But I have been with him long. A long long time for Peregrina."

"We'd better mount up again. The sooner we're away the safer."

"Yes. We must not be caught. I must have my revenge."

I DID NOT THINK IT of him. I did not think him capable of that. And what will they do with poor little Liese? Conrad lay still and awake on his bed for a long time while the alarm bell rang and rang.

At work, he and Kutta took over the second conference room and he explained as Kutta worked with the new demonstration module. The room was set up with rear-projection on an inbuilt wall screen, and the giant ghostly images shifted and flickered while Kutta operated his laptop.

It worked well.

"This seems good," Kutta said after a while. "Let me work up a presentation and we'll round up some of our non-product people and see how it goes."

"Maybe Lydia."

"Of course Lydia. I'd like to rope in some accounting and payroll types too. They're always complaining that they're so busy, and it'll be fun to make them suffer."

"Who else don't we like?"

"Nah, I want a friendly audience."

"Ask Lydia to choose. She knows everyone's schedule."

"Not bad. You like Lydia, don't you?"

"Everybody likes Lydia."

"Not the women."

They laughed.

Next day, Lagonigro made a rare appearance in the break room as Conrad ate his lunch.

"Say, Sal," Conrad called. "What's all this about a move to Texas?"

Everyone in the room stopped moving. Conrad couldn't swear to it, but he thought he heard a concerted gasp, as from half a dozen intakes of breath, separate and sudden.

"What?"

"Texas. I keep hearing a rumor we're moving to Texas."

"Where did you hear that?"

"Oh, hither and yon. Have you heard anything?"

Lagonigro shook his head.

"That's above my pay grade."

"My friend ..."

"I just do numbers."

He was clearly lying. Any move to Texas would cost money, and anything that cost money would fall under his purview.

Lagonigro did not take his lunch in the break room that day, but then he almost never did.

One by one, as the others finished their lunches and left the room, they each clapped Conrad on the shoulder. Congratulating him for his great deed.

For the next few days, Conrad was beset by unaccustomed worries. What would happen to Liese? She was no part of Flik-Flak's plans, he was sure. Would he simply pitch her in the river? Even after Flik-Flak's treachery, Conrad could not believe him capable of that. It would not burnish his reputation. It would have no style. Besides, if he really intended to marry the Gräfin Mittelsbach, surely it would behoove him not to upset her with an act of such barbarity.

Still, he wondered what was happening in his absence. And as he wondered, another thought struck him. *Was* he absent? Was he not there by the river as well as here at Business Data Intercontinental? Were there two Conrads? Or was a doppelgänger of some sort carrying on, holding his place until his return? These and similar questions he found quite beyond his powers. So he pondered, and worried, as he went about his mundane daily tasks.

For a while the new demo was out of his hands. Kutta was working on his presentation, and the second conference room was reserved for next Tuesday. Already they had six lined up for the audience, Lydia among them, and, surprisingly, Herrick. Conrad wondered if Herrick too was finding himself with more free time than was comfortable. Himself, he had been scheduled to go out on another demo on Thursday, this time to a financial services firm, but they cancelled at the last minute and he found himself scrambling to invent enough plausible tasks to fill up the remainder of his week and to remain inconspicuous to management.

On Friday, the day for dumping bad news, Mr. Noakes called a very peculiar meeting. He announced a new initiative, "Generation Data," that was going to bring a more agile, responsive company into the era of fourth-generation technology. Whatever that was. There were handouts, so Conrad didn't bother to take notes. Instead, he watched the faces of his coworkers. Some of the new hires, tech geeks all, looked excited. Among the old hands, Conrad could tell who had been "in the know," whose input had been solicited. The others, the people like him—Conrad could see them struggle to keep the skepticism, tinged with contempt, off their faces. Herrick was one of these. As time went on, their expressions froze into foreboding.

Kutta, interestingly enough, was unreadable.

"All of us need to examine our own responsibilities, our own challenges, in light of the priorities listed in the Strategic Planning Document. What can we do to help bring BDI" (they were renaming Business Data Intercontinental) "where we need to go? Nobody knows your positions and responsibilities better than you. No one can do a better job than you projecting where you fit in at BDI 2012."

There were to be Team Leaders, one for each department, who would manage all the fact-finding and brainstorming. They would "aggregate the ideas and perspectives" presented by their team members, and bring the results to the Divisional Pathfinders.

"Remember, these are not going to be complaint sessions. I don't want to hear about what you don't like about your job *now* what you want changed *now*. Everything is oriented to the future. What we are going to be ... what you are going to be ... what BDI is going to be."

What a waste. Conrad was convinced that all the major changes had already been decided upon, mostly by people who were not in this room. But least the boss had said oriented, not "orientated." Conrad could be grateful for that.

The meeting broke up. Those in-the-know stayed behind in the first conference room with the door open and chatted. The rest drifted off to their work stations, exchanging a few cryptic comments.

"What do you think?" Herrick asked.

"Looks like trouble."

"That's what I think. But I guess something had to be done."

"There may be trouble ahead ..." Bobby K sang.

Some of them went out for drinks after work. Years ago Conrad would have been among them, but not now. Nobody asked, and he was not sorry they didn't. Nothing had been said about a move, the only topic that interested Conrad. For the rest of it, if he fit in anywhere in 2012, it probably wasn't going to be at BDI.

HE AWOKE IN WHAT SEEMED to be a barn, lying in a bank of straw with Peregrina by his side. She had awakened first and was sitting up, combing her fingers through her thick auburn hair, pulling out stray wisps of straw and whatever else. It was still dark.

Peregrina turned over her shoulder and addressed Conrad.

"Today we will reach Dachsburg. I have friends there. Perhaps they can tell us where Flik-Flak has gone. He has been often at Dachsburg."

"Would they tell us?"

"They would tell me."

She stood up and straightened her clothes.

"Did you sleep well?" she asked.

"I think so. I am not tired."

"Good. We should leave. The farmers will come soon."

Conrad jumped to his feet. As he buckled on his sword, he became aware of a drumming noise.

"Do you hear that?"

Peregrina went to the door and swung it open a few degrees.

"Ach, rain. A torrent. We cannot walk in this."

Conrad joined her, looking out the door, looking past her at the new streams of water flowing past the barn.

"I think it won't last," he said.

"We must climb up and hide. It would go against my heart to harm the farmers."

"Perhaps they will not come. Perhaps they will wait for the rain to stop."

"It is easy to see you have never been a farmer," Peregrina smiled. "They will come."

They climbed up to the next level and found a good place for a nest back near the wall. Even if someone came up the ladder, they would not be seen unless they were deliberately searched for. They could hear after a while the animals stomping and blowing while the farmers brought their feed and did whatever it is farmers do. The rain was loud against the roof.

Conrad leaned to Peregrina and spoke in a whisper.

"You promised last night that you would tell me. What does Flik-Flak want with the unfortunate Gräfin? I cannot believe he is following his heart, not away from the lady Peregrina."

Peregrina puffed, a sound of contempt.

"Flik-Flak has a heart only for adventure and outrage not for love. No, it is the inheritance he is after, the treasure that goes with the lady's hand."

"I did not think he was so venal."

"I forget you are a foreigner. You do not know the story. The gold and the jewels and the fine silver plate would mean little to him, apart from the getting of them. No, what he is after, what the black Baron of Reichenstein desired, is the right to the Three Treasures of the Mittelsbachs."

"Ah, the Three Treasures." Conrad nodded. "What might those be?"

"The Three Treasures are the banner, the ring and the horn. Their virtues are these, so says the dwarf who gave them to the first Mittelsbach all those many years ago. The Red Banner–whoever carries it to battle will bear the victory, despite any odds. The Ring, set with an emerald stone, gives the power to him who wears it of reading the thoughts of men. The Horn calls aid from a far country, another time another place, a land of faerie."

"So. It is these that Flik-Flak covets."

"He wishes to be known as the possessor and wielder of the gifts. To increase his worship. For me, I do not believe he covets the power of the gifts as would many another. As does the Baron. Flik-Flak cares little for victory or defeat, only for the game and that it continue."

"I think perhaps you miss him a little."

"You shall see how I miss him when we come together again."

"It surprises me that with these great gifts that the Mittelsbachs have not been ... a greater name, a greater power."

"They are wise. They have been sparing, very sparing in the use of the gifts. There are conditions as well, there are always conditions that attach to such enchantments. Three times only each gift can be used. The Banner has been used twice already, once before it came to the Mittelsbachs and once by the fifth count to break the Long Siege. The Ring has been used once, in the service of the emperor, to save his life in foreign lands. The Horn has never been sounded."

"An interesting tale," said Conrad. "Do you believe it?"

"Of course. The victory was won, the emperor was saved."

Conrad lay in the straw and looked at the barn roof, admiring the joinings. After a time he spoke.

"Listen."

"I hear nothing."

"The rain has stopped. The farmers have gone."

Peregrina rose again and again brushed off the hay from where it clung. She clapped on her travelling hat, and swiveled her shortsword to its accustomed place on her hip. Without a word they climbed down from the loft and made for the door. A pause; a listen. Then out the door, around the barn and straight for the woods, keeping the barn between themselves and the main house. It was good to get out of the mud surrounding the barn. They were seen, Conrad was sure, by a man under a wide-brimmed hat driving a cart, but he had trouble enough with the soaking from the rain and the muddy slipping road, and he gave no sign.

Soon they were under the shadow of the trees, in a leaf-paved lane. Peregrina knew the road, it was clear. The path began to climb.

THE PRACTICE DEMONSTRATION was over. Conrad found there had been nothing for him to do; he no longer had a part in the actual show, only in the preparation. He made a note to himself to include that in his Generation Data report. He spent the time observing the little group of guinea pigs they had collected. Some, the clerical workers and whatnot, zoned out after a brief struggle. The flesh was willing but the spirit was weak. There was a little curly-haired blonde who did data entry for Human Resources whose frowning face was the picture of woe. She reminded Conrad irresistibly of Liese on the raft, though of course the circumstances were not so dire.

Lydia and Herrick held together best, engaging with Kutta throughout, asking the best questions they could generate. The problem was, since neither of them had any personal use for the database nor could conceive of what use there might be, their questions were not really pertinent. Kutta didn't mind. He told Conrad later: "Half the people at a real demonstration don't know what's going on. They're just there to represent their departments or fill up seats. I still have to deal with them."

Kutta did well. When he ran into a problem, or a question he couldn't answer, he rattled off a canned reply that sounded sincere, something along the lines of, "That's interesting, that's an issue that hasn't come up before, let me look into that when I get back to the office and I'll email you," and carried on.

When the demo was over, Kutta closed the program, and the wall screen showed his laptop background, a picture of an aspirational vehicle, Conrad thought maybe a Lamborghini.

"OK, that's it. Thank you all for being here. Any further queries, suggestions, questions? Anyone ... anyone ... Bueller?"

"I thought it was good," Lydia said. "I don't know anything about Economics, but it looked impressive."

Lydia swiveled in her chair, hooking an elbow over the back, looking at the others for confirmation. She had a fine strong back, very solid. She was thicker than she had at first appeared. She dressed in a way such as to minimize it, with a lot of loose flowy scarves and things. Conrad found himself favorably impressed by that fine strong back.

"Out for drinks after work at Julio's? My treat," said Kutta.

And most of them whined, it was Tuesday, it was the middle of the week, they had this and they had that.

"Hey, I gotta go to work too. I'm not gonna make a night of it."

No takers. Soon they had all cleared out except Kutta, Conrad, and Herrick, who was obviously waiting to make a last comment.

"You might run into problems with the firewall at some of these colleges or universities. Some of them have weird setups. A lot of time they have to make a specific exception to let a database through."

"Good point. I'll have to call ahead and make sure someone takes care of that. You up for drinks?"

"Can't do it tonight. Tuesdays and Thursday are out."

"No one can make it. Screw it. Maybe on Friday. I'll send an email."

Chapter 4

TWO MEN EXCHANGED GLANCES across a wood plank table. Thunderstruck, or so they seemed.

"Flik-Flak did that? To you? To Peregrina?"

"He did."

"Perhaps you were mistaken in some way. Are you sure?"

"Such a question! Was I not there? Am I a fool?"

"It does not seem like him."

"Not like him? When has he brooked at betrayal? Have you not heard him call treachery one of the dark arts?"

"But against Peregrina? I thought you were his destiny. I thought that he would stay with you forever."

"Perhaps that is why he did what he did. No matter. This man was with me and has remained with me. He seeks the Lady of Mittelsbach. I seek Flik-Flak. Will you help us?"

The men were silent for a moment, and took council with their steins. They were close enough in looks that they might be brothers. Conrad's clear impression was of their unspoken admiration for Flik-Flak's audacity. He felt that they would not help Peregrina.

"Honored lady, I don't know what we can do," said the one named Dieter, whom Conrad judged to be the older of the two. A bearded strongly-built man of peasant stock who had taken to the roving life somewhere along his life's line and never returned to field and farm.

"You can tell me where he went."

"How would we know that?"

"Was he not here?"

Here was a long pause. They judged the chances of a successful lie and decided against the attempt.

"Of course, yes, he was here. He stayed briefly, a few days, the passage of two nights only. But he told us nothing of his plans."

"Was the woman with him?"

"Two women. The countess one. A woman of great beauty and obvious refinement." It was the younger man, Petrus, speaking now. Conrad judged that he was a student seduced into the life of an adventurer. A bit taller, a bit slenderer than Dieter, but otherwise, peas in a pod, happy in their new life. "Her fine clothes were the worse for travel and rain."

"The other a delightful morsel," said Dieter. "A little blonde, young and fresh, but so distressed it wrung my heart I assure you."

Petrus was watching Conrad.

"Flik-Flak kept the ladies apart from us," he said. "So Dieter had no opportunity to comfort the maiden."

"And he told you nothing of who they were?" Peregrina asked.

"He gave them names. What were they now ...?"

"I do not recall," said Dieter. "Others might know. We called them Rose Red and Snow White."

Peregrina sat and regarded them, arms crossed tight over her famous and admirable bosom, breathing fire.

"So, Peregrina at last finds out who her friends are."

"My lady, my lady, if we but knew ..."

"You heard no reports from elsewhere?" Conrad broke in. "You did not guess who the ladies were? The rescue has been noised up and down the river."

"Rumor came, but only on the second day. We are somewhat isolated here. Perhaps that was why Flik-Flak left when he did."

They were in Dachsburg, not a town as Conrad had expected, but an almost inaccessible lair set midst the rocks and narrow wooded valleys far to the north of Castle Reichenstein. There were no villages or farms in this wilderness, not the sight nor the sound of a dwelling. It was an ancient stone ruin in a trackless waste, built and inhabited long ago by a tribe long departed. Fragments of stone walls rose out of the ground, some tall like spires reaching toward the sky. It reminded Conrad somewhat of an old Italian painting of the nativity, where the birth occurred against the wall of a ruin rather than in the more familiar stable.

The bandits had found the place and made it their own, set it up with whatever comfort a bandit would need, a roof here, a bed and a table there, a good fire for warmth. They were always coming and going, swapping tales of the road, sharing news. It was a very clearing house for banditry. There were only a few in residence at the moment; besides Petrus and Dieter, a couple more sitting over straw on the stone floor, leaning against a half-wall, sharing a jug and a loaf and watching Peregrina from a distance.

At length Peregrina turned away from Petrus and Dieter.

"Well you cannot tell what you will not. Or what you don't know," she conceded grudgingly. "Perhaps it was too much to hope that Flik-Flak would reveal his plans even here. He knew he would be pursued, and the art of treachery is practiced by others as well as himself. Come, let us find a berth. We might as well spend the night here."

They found a stone cubby, enclosed on three sides, covered over at one end by thickly woven branches. They had to duck to fit under the makeshift roof. Conrad thought it might once have been a place for the storage of grain or wine.

"There is one thing," he said as he arranged his sleeping sack on the ground. "We know now that they passed through here, and not long ago."

"That is true." Peregrina stretched over a long red blanket, ready to fold herself in like a crepe. "But where afterwards? And who can I ask next? I had hoped for more from Dachsburg."

They had scarcely made up their beds when they heard feet running outside and urgent voices. Two new men had come up the trail into camp and the others were gathering round.

"Quick, quick, the Brotherhood. They are close behind."

"You were followed?" Dieter asked.

"Nonsense. We found them gathered in the valley below, at the crossroads. We hurried here by the Robber Road to warn you."

"Well done. How many?"

"I made a dozen at least. Too many to fight. They are coming with purpose. What do they want with us, we have nothing to do with the Brotherhood?"

Then he saw Peregrina.

"My lady Peregrina!" he said. "Is then Flik-Flak here?"

"He is not," she said.

"We have no time to explain," said Petrus. "We must scatter."

Four men, the two who had brought the alarm and the two who a few moments ago had been eating and drinking at their ease, turned without a word and simply flowed through, around, and over the stones of the ruin and off into the trees beyond, travelling by paths long prepared, but invisible to the uninitiated.

"Peregrina and her companion, come with us by the Chimney, Peregrina first. Hurry!"

They could hear the knights of the Brotherhood approaching, on foot but with great rapidity, as if making their last rush.

The Chimney, it transpired, was an unobtrusive opening in the base of an ancient hearth, but an opening that led below for the escape of people, not above for the escape of smoke. They stepped around and behind the high, built-up fire that was burning in the center of the hearth and climbed, one after another, into the hole. Down, down they climbed, a tunnel stretching straight down, sometimes surrounded by shaped and mortared stones, sometimes through the hewn native rock, clinging to handholds and footholds, metal loops driven into the walls many years ago. Conrad's feet kept slipping and he had to leave a great deal of space between himself and Peregrina to avoid kicking her in the head. Still they descended. There was some light in the tunnel, some subtle openings made to the outside world, but the tunnel was dim at the best of times, and now, with twilight falling, it was hard indeed to discern the black metal holds in the reddening light. Still they descended, the only sound the scraping of feet and the heavy raking breaths of the climbers. It seemed impossible. It seemed that they must already be below the level of the valley floor, below the river bed. But still they went on. It seemed impossible. But then again it was a dream, was it not?

CONRAD WAS SURPRISED to find, sitting beside him at the bar, Charlotte, the little curly-haired blonde from the practice demo. Kutta, never one to give up on a design, had reconvened the after-demo celebration at Julio's on Friday. Although with one proviso.

"You all gotta pay your own way. I can foot the bill for an after-work Tuesday sippage, but not for a Friday blowout. You're on your own today."

It was quite a gathering. With all the uncertainty surrounding the possible move and the restructuring, people seemed ready to relax, and to relax together. Conrad was surprised to see Charlotte with them, as she had always seemed rather shy, but she was probably just as surprised to see him there, as he had always seemed, so he imagined, indifferent to his coworkers. It had been a long time since anything had gotten in the way of his straight walk out to the lot and straight drive home.

Herrick was there, talking to Kutta. Lydia was not there, a fact Kutta and Conrad noticed simultaneously.

"Hey! Where's Lydia?"

"I think she's going out with Sal," said Charlotte, then immediately ducked her head as if she regretted making the observation.

"What? Lydia and Lagonigro? An unholy alliance?"

"I don't know I'd call it an alliance ..." began one of the other office women, an older, somewhat motherly type, though she would not have been happy to hear herself described as such.

"It's an alliance," insisted Kutta. "If it's Lagonigro, it's an alliance. The Consigliere. We're toast if those two get together. Between them they control everything in the office. They can destroy us one by one. We've got to split them up. How 'bout it, Conrad?" He came over and put his hands on Conrad's shoulders, kneading his upper trapezius. "You wanna volunteer to break them up?"

Charlotte giggled a trifle nervously.

"I never interfere in such matters of the heart."

"Heart? Lagonigro?"

"I'm afraid Lydia is on her own."

"That's just the point. She's not on her own."

Kutta laughed immoderately at his own jest and wandered off down the bar.

Charlotte was sipping some kind of newfangled blue girly-looking drink whose properties she discussed with another workmate, a girl seated on her other side. Conrad leaned towards them and listened in.

Charlotte told him the name of the drink and he forgot as soon as he heard it.

"Did you ever try it?"

"No. I generally stick to a few old favorites."

"What's that?"

"An old-fashioned."

They discussed the old-fashioned. She seemed interested. They continued talking. She talked easily. She did not move away in a few minutes to talk to younger more interesting people, as Conrad had come to expect.

She was telling him now how she had found herself doing data entry for HR.

"I used to be an accountant. I studied to be an accountant. I was always good at math."

"That's a good trade," said Conrad, although he didn't know that it was.

"Mmph." Charlotte made a sound indicative of deep skepticism supported by painful experience. "I didn't like it. I only lasted a year and a half. The pressure around tax time was too much. A lot of screaming. At me. Maybe it was the firm I worked at. But I didn't want to even try another one. I got a job here with payroll."

"I thought you with Human Resources."

"They transferred me there. It's supposed to be temporary. We'll see. They needed help in HR."

"That sounds ominous. At least your skills are transferrable if the company closes offices or moves."

"Blecch."

Conrad laughed.

"Indeed."

"Do you think they will? Move, I mean."

"It's really hard to say. I'm inclined to think no because they don't have any other branch offices in the area. They may trim staff. It's hard to say. This whole 'Generation Data' thing ... what did they call it? an initiative? ... has me thinking, though. I don't think they'd go through all that without having something big in mind."

"I hope we don't move. I like it here."

"You like New York?"

"I grew up here." Charlotte looked around furtively. "I still live with my parents. In my old room. Isn't that sad?"

"I don't think it's sad. What's sad about it? I still live I my old house where I grew up. I don't how people can afford to live in New York otherwise. I mean ordinary people."

"Everyone is always telling me I should move out."

"Are they going to pay your rent? Or your parents' upkeep? I mean the upkeep on the house."

They laughed. Most everyone else had gone home. They moved to a table and got a burger and a salad. The burger was Conrad's. They listened to the piped music, most from the sixties and seventies. She was very good at guessing names and titles.

"It's funny," Conrad observed. "So many places play oldies now. When I was young, when you'd go out to a bar or restaurant they wouldn't be playing the Andrews Sisters or anything analogously old."

"People like oldies."

Conrad was not surprised that she was a native New Yorker. There was a certain naïveté in her that he recognized. Children of the city growing up and staying in the same neighborhood, in Queens or the Bronx or Brooklyn or Staten Island, shopping at the same stores for years, attending the same schools their parents had attended, going to the same churches all their lives, they were like small-town girls and boys. Very different from the newcomers who arrived looking for trouble, attracted by New York's flashy media image.

She was very young. When the time came to break the party up and go home, she pulled out a cell phone and readied a call to her father, to pick her up. It was no surprise to Conrad that she didn't drive.

"Don't be silly. I'll drive you."

"I'm not sure I know the way from here. Do you have a GPS?"

"Don't be silly."

"We could use the map function on my phone."

Conrad opened his mouth to speak, but Charlotte forestalled him.

"OK, OK. I won't be silly."

There was no GPS along the banks of the river, Conrad thought grimly. No cell phones in Burg Reichenstein.

When she climbed into the passenger seat, a fresh neat young person, Conrad was conscious of the shabbiness of his old car and by extension of himself. Surprised, but not displeased. This is how we go, he thought. This is how we have always gone.

Although she gave him the address, Conrad didn't know the way to Charlotte's house any better than she did. He drove back toward the Business Data offices, and as soon as they got close she said, "Oh, I know where we are," and commenced giving efficient direction.

They dipped down onto the parkway. She lived south of the office, along Conrad's usual route home. When she directed him off the parkway back into the side streets he felt a sudden thrill of incipient recognition, and when they crossed the overpass to the left he was sure. This was the very neighborhood where he had seen the horseman riding up the slope, where he had later seen the Brotherhood gathering, disguised as city workers. He gripped the steering wheel, on high alert. This was no accident. This was intended.

"THERE ARE MORE COMING. Three rode in just now."

Peregrina was standing in front of the window. They were in a spacious bedroom in an inn, a room with plastered walls and heavy dark beams at odd angles under a slanting roof. They were on the third floor, and Peregrina was watching the street below. Conrad was lying in bed, watching Peregrina, her thick auburn hair falling over her unbuttoned back.

"We did right to come here," said Conrad.

"It goes against my heart and my practice to pay for lodging," said Peregrina.

"It is a good place to watch from." Conrad joined her at the window.

"How many now *in toto*?" he asked.

"Six. The three who came last night and the three who rode in just now. They must have heard something. We were wise to follow them. That was a good thought on your part."

They stood together, looking down at another inn across the street. Lightly tethered to a hitching post out front, three fine horses, newly arrived, sported the livery of the Brotherhood.

As they watched, two black knights stepped from the opposite inn door, accompanied by a groom. Peregrina instinctively took a half-step back.

"I am known here," she said. "That is both good and bad. Many friends but some enemies. Some friends that may prove themselves enemies in the face of gold or steel. My part in the Countess's escape from Reichenstein is well known. The Brotherhood would pay well for news of me. I think that it would be wiser not to go abroad during the day. At night, in the dark, there are places I can go where I will be safe."

"I'll go and find what I can," said Conrad. "Those three knights of the Brotherhood who waylaid me by the riverside are dead. There is no reason for anyone to know me here. Let me walk up and down the streets and wharfs and see what I can find. See if the Brotherhood have made inquiries that betray their plans."

Peregrina nodded.

"Good. Come back at sundown. I will have our meal sent up."

"Our first parting since the treachery of Flik-Flak." Conrad smiled. "While I am gone, you can catch up on your sleep."

Conrad swung down along the cramped and twisted stairwell by the aid of the occasional exposed beam, then stepped into the noise of the open street. It was a good town, this town, a hub, with bustling river traffic and good roads leading inland. They were out of the high hilly country, and commerce passed freely in all directions. After all those days on the road, Conrad was glad to be a townsman again. He took a deep breath and savored the thousand smells of the street.

When it comes down to it, I am no detective, he thought. But at the very least, I can see the town.

He took a seat on the edge of a great fountain that stood in the center of the broad, cobbled main street. The low, lipped stone wall on which Conrad sat contained a wide pool of clear potable water, and in the center of the pool a larger-than-life statue of a milkmaid stood on tumbled rocks, ceaselessly spilling from her stone pail. She was the pride of Neustadt—many hundreds of years old was that town, but Neustadt was its name—and her fountain was a favorite gathering place of the people.

For a long time Conrad sat and watched the flow of life, passing a word or two with the townsfolk when he saw the opportunity, trying to sense patterns of disturbance or excitement. Once three of the black Brotherhood came and stood for a while talking in the shadow of the milkmaid, and Conrad strained to hear them. He could make nothing of their conversation, only that they were hunting someone. But that he knew already.

At length he began his walk up and down the street, stopping wherever he thought people would gather. He bought a silk handkerchief and a wallet and flowers and snuff although he did not use it. For people are more apt to talk to a customer than to a mere passerby.

He ate two lunches and drank many pots of ale. He learned a great deal about the Brotherhood. There were six, nine, even twelve in town. They were going on to Eckenfluss; they were crossing the river tonight; they were headed back to Burg Reichenstein having given up the pursuit. They were gathering at Neustadt, and when they had mustered sufficient strength, they would lead an assault against the Countess's palace at Mittelsbach. Conrad thought that no one knew the Brotherhood's plans and he began to suspect that the Brotherhood themselves had not decided on their next move.

Late afternoon saw a sleepy Conrad walking along the river's edge. He had unwittingly neglected the most important section of Neustadt. The river traffic was the life blood of the town and there were many men engaged in the business of guiding boats to shore and bringing cargo onto land. A thought occurred to Conrad, late in the day.

He called to a big man supervising the rolling of great tuns of sweet river wine off a barge and onto a wooden wharf.

"Excuse me, good sir. Do you know where I could find a ferry to take me over the river?"

The big man looked annoyed. Perhaps Conrad had adopted a condescending tone without realizing it. The man simply pointed north, downriver, and went back to his business.

A hundred yards or so further on, Conrad found what he was looking for. A number of flat river boats were gathered near a large freestanding structure, basically a peaked roof sitting on pillars. As he watched, five or six passengers with wheelbarrows and hand carts filed aboard a small boat that was getting ready to cast off. Conrad walked among the other captains inquiring about passage, but all claimed to be already hired for the afternoon, although they stood empty at the time.

"*Herr Blumen, Herr Blumen.*"

Conrad heard a voice calling and turned. A short, broad man of middle age, unshaven and somewhat savage-looking, was beckoning to him.

At first he was insulted, but then he remembered the flowers he had purchased and affixed to his cloak for want of a better place to put them.

"You are calling me?"

"You want passage over the river?"

"I may want a passage soon."

"I can row you over. I have a rowboat. You have companions?"

"One only."

"These others will not help you. They are engaged. But I carry men, not birds. Look."

Groomsmen were leading three great dark horses, horses draped in black livery, onto the largest of the ferries. Three, thought Conrad, always they travel in threes.

"You see? I have nothing to do with the Brotherhood of the Raven."

Conrad thought, if they are loading now, they must be planning to cross soon, before dark.

He said, "Can you wait? It may be some time, the matter of an hour or more, before I return."

"Of course. Have I your word?"

"I will come back to pay passage, that I promise."

He ran along the quay, looking for gap in the buildings where he could return to the main street. When he found a narrow opening, passing between steep cross-gabled buildings, he discovered that he was almost directly opposite the inn where he and Peregrina had found lodging.

He burst into their room and found Peregrina sitting on a chair near the window combing out her hair in the late afternoon sunlight, looking scrubbed and shiny and magnificent.

"I have had a bath," she said. "I recommend it. And my clothes are drying, all but this shift." She picked up the white corner. "I saw you walking throughout the town and now you come running back. You have news?"

"The Brotherhood is crossing the river. I saw their horses loading. I have engaged a boatman to ferry us over."

"Ach. I have ordered our food already."

"I'll go down to the kitchen and have them pack it for us. Your clothes, how wet are they?"

"Damp still. But I can cobble together enough to wear. But there is yet a problem. I cannot go abroad while the sun shines. For sure I would be recognized, by the Brotherhood and by others."

"We must get you a cloak and a hood. It pains me to say it, but we must cover you up again, head and body. The ferryman will not betray us, he hates the Brotherhood. Or so he has said, and I believe him. But we must go now."

He rushed from the room.

Chapter 5

ROUND AND ROUND AND up and down Conrad drove, looking for a place to park. The narrow streets were poorly marked. Once he was fooled by a one-way alley, and had to back halfway up the block in the face of a furious truck. He found at last metered student parking, a small number of spaces angled into the curb. As it was Saturday, there were spaces free, and he pulled the car in, then raided his door compartment for quarters.

This was the hub, the neighborhood where everything converged: the white horse, the Brotherhood in disguise, Charlotte's humble home, and now this elegant mysterious house, which Conrad couldn't help but view as the Countess' waking-world palace. This is where he would see ... whatever there was to be seen.

It was this way.

When he drove Charlotte home after drinks and dinner at Julio's, he had recognized the neighborhood as soon as they pulled up out of the parkway. This was where he had seen those anomalous sights that seemed to connect to his dream. It could not be a coincidence that he had been drawn here now, that Charlotte lived here.

Sure enough, when they crossed the parkway and tried to make their way toward Charlotte's house, they were blocked. There were police cars standing in the road, with the party lights flashing, and a number of dark figures spread across the street and sidewalk. Conrad perceived that they were concentrating on a particular house, a small, old, rather elegant structure holding its own among the tall brown brick buildings.

"Oh my gosh, this again," said Charlotte.

"What is this?"

"There's always some kind of trouble here. They're always protesting outside this house."

"Why?"

"The lady who lives here runs a museum a couple of days a week. It's a really old house. Her family has lived here since forever. Her great-grandfather or something was a silversmith who came over from Germany. She has antique silver creamers and ewers and things displayed all over the house. And her great-grandmother was a seamstress so she has all these beautiful old silk gowns standing on frames. And all the old furniture and things. I don't think she's changed anything for a century."

"And people don't like that? What are they protesting? Don't they like Germans around here?"

Charlotte laughed.

"No, they've had a lot of beefs over the years. Supposedly there are code violations, something to do with safety or access. But my father says it's all a pretext."

"For what?"

"They want to expand the Muni Uni campus. Everything else is apartments, she's the only house. So the students are always protesting. Of course, they've managed to bring racial stuff into it. Fight the power. You know. Plus the developers stand to make a pile of money if they can get her to sell out or move."

"Is this what they're calling eminent domain now?"

"I don't know. My father thinks the land developers are behind most of it. Anyway, she's not going anywhere if she can help it." Charlotte turned and looked out the rear window. "Do you want to back up and go another way?"

"This looks like it's clearing up. I wouldn't mind waiting. If it's OK with you," he added.

Charlotte rocked her head in an easy assent.

"OK."

Then she said, "I feel sorry for her. She's only one person. One lonely old woman. I used to go visit her museum sometimes. I never saw more than one or two people there. It was really quiet. I liked it. She liked me. She wanted me to help out around the place. I went a few times. She was quiet too. It's like she belonged there, somewhere back in the past, with the house and her great-grandparents."

They watched the student protesters move off the street and off the besieged lady's front steps. They had brought their own cameras to record themselves.

"I didn't stay long. There wasn't enough work."

"What's her name?"

"Diana Lind. I used to call her Lady Diana. To myself."

The street was clear, the police cars had pulled to the side. Conrad began rolling slowly forward.

"Look, there she is!"

Conrad looked up and saw, standing on the lit stoop, a dark-haired distressed woman speaking to a police officer. Not an old woman, except in the eyes of a child. He stopped. The woman noticed and looked up and the policeman looked around. Conrad held his gaze as long as he could. Then he started forward again.

He brought Charlotte to her house and watched her until the door opened and she turned to give him the customary farewell wave. But all the while he was thinking of the woman on the stoop, Lady Diana. Tomorrow, he would return.

So now tomorrow had come, a Saturday, and he was walking from his parking place at Muni Uni to the museum house, the palace. He stopped a couple of times and consulted a street map, old enough to be frayed at the folds and even gapped in places. The distance was deceiving, but he kept on and found the right cross street at the bottom of a short hill.

Here now was the house, surrounded indeed, by greater, taller, duller buildings to an extent he had not appreciated in the dark. There was a narrow strip of land on either side of the house, maybe the width of a garbage pail, protected from the street by a short length of wrought iron fencing, crowned by spikes. The wrought iron motif continued up the front steps, an almost delicate iron railing on either side of what looked to be sandstone. He stopped on the sidewalk and looked up at the house.

He saw bay windows with many tiny panes of glass, three narrow stories of dark clapboard with dormers on top, sprouting from red shingles. An elegant little structure, to be sure, and very well kept. But the sidewalk, he now saw, was defaced with paint and chalk, and the sandstone of the steps was similarly marked, and scratched in places, even chipped, as if by impotent imps striving to do harm.

Conrad climbed the steps and faced the door, tight shut. He nosed along the landing and found, in large gold lettering over beveled glass panes, the museum's hours. It was open only two days a week, Wednesdays and Thursdays. This was a disappointment.

He considered his move. Should he knock? Some saving touch of sanity told him no. Would she even recognize him? Perhaps she would be confused and alarmed. It would be better to come back during regular museum hours, to ease gradually into introductions and revelations. She had been pressed enough lately. Better let her be.

He retreated down the stairs and headed back toward his car. No sooner had he reached the top of the first short hill than he heard his name being called. He turned and saw Charlotte looking at him with an odd expression on her face. She was carrying groceries.

"Conrad! What are you doing here?"

"I came to visit the museum. You know the German silver museum. Lady Diana's."

"Is that even still open?"

"The sign said Wednesdays and Thursdays."

"Too bad. You should have called ahead."

"I couldn't find a phone number or a website. As a matter of fact, I couldn't find any reference to the place online anywhere."

"Yeah, I don't imagine she has a website."

There was a brief silence.

"Well, I better get back," Conrad said. "It's a drag driving this same old route on my day off. At least the traffic's lighter."

"OK. See you on Monday."

They parted.

"THE LADY IS TIRED? She wishes to rest?"

They'd found lodgings with a woodsman, and the few pennies they paid for their keep was a welcome boon to his household.

"Yes. I will be staying in my room today," said Peregrina.

The lady was not tired. She was a better traveler than Conrad himself. It was the old trouble, the fear of being recognized, especially here in Wand'rerstand.

Wand'rerstand had been founded many years ago, as a staging place for the emperor's messengers. There had been a network of such places all over the empire, where horses were kept in readiness along with fodder and water and supplies. Little more than fortified blockhouses at first, they increased in splendor along with the emperor's servants. They were safe havens set among the rough places of the empire, and they were welcomed by the local inhabitants. Soon little towns had sprung up around them, inns where other travelers could mingle with the imperial messengers, blacksmith's shops, armorers, launderers, seamstresses, bakeries, one built on another. Now, as the great wave of the empire started to recede, many of the imperial stages were falling into disuse. Wand'rerstand was one of the few to retain its former glory.

"I will go to the Stand and wait for Günther," Conrad said for the benefit of the woodsman and his wife, and gave Peregrina a chaste husbandly kiss. There would be no "Günther" arriving, but it gave them a reason to stay for a few days.

They were well away from the river here, and the land was densely wooded and shaped into low gentle hills. Conrad enjoyed his walk through the cool of the trees, a few hundred yards of shade and quiet before he came out at the head of the town. Wand'rerstand was a single cobblestone street sloping gently down to the two main buildings at the base, the blockhouse for the emperor's men and the inn facing it. At the top of the slope to Conrad's right, stood one square tower of middle height above a walled courtyard. Chickens clucked and bobbed in and out of the yard. White fluttering clothes dried on a line projecting from a second story window. Conrad stood for a moment looking at the scene and took a satisfied sighing breath, then continued down the street.

It was to be another day of waiting and watching. Their plan had come to nothing. They'd followed a dozen of the Brotherhood's knights from the left bank of the river, convinced that they were hot on Flik-Flak's trail, but when the knights came to Wand'rerstand they scattered to the points of the compass, and left Conrad and Peregrina baffled. It seemed they had failed.

As he approached the bottom of the road, Conrad saw three of the emperor's men crossing in front of him from the blockhouse to the inn, probably intending there to rest and to eat and to drink while their new horses were being prepared. They were recognized by the golden eagle across their chests, and by the archaic cut of their clothes, down to the old-fashioned riding trousers and boots wrapped up the leg with leather cords, the way they had been since the messenger corps was founded a long age before.

Conrad fell easily in behind them and followed them to the inn. At the entrance they suddenly stopped in front of him. Conrad could just see over their shoulders into the doorway, and in the smoky darkness he saw the shapes of a number of Brothers of the Raven blocking the way. For a long moment, neither would yield.

There was no love lost between the Brotherhood and the emperor's Eagle Messengers. It is natural for an empire to find any lesser loyalty suspect at best and treasonous at worst, and the Brotherhood made no reports to the emperor. The brothers' loyalty was to one another only and to their guild, though their ultimate purpose remained something of a mystery. They were a relatively new society, and as the reach of the empire grew shorter and the appearance of its agents grew less frequent and more remarkable, the power and heft of the Brotherhood seemed to grow. There had been, so far as Conrad knew, as yet no open conflict between them, but here they stood, facing each other under the lintel, and no one was taking a backward step.

Then all at once, one of the brothers stepped to the side and waved the messengers through with an expansive gesture. Even in his poor viewing conditions, Conrad could see an elaborate sarcasm in the motion. The messengers passed through first; Conrad waited to let the brothers pass and as they did, he heard one pass a remark to the others, and following that, loud—purposely loud—laughter. Inside the inn, the last of the messengers turned back to the doorway with an angry look. There would be trouble between them soon, these two powers, Conrad was sure of it.

He sat down at the bar and looked around the tap room as his eyes got used to the light. Aside from the messengers, there were only ordinary travelers like himself, about their own business. He recognized no one. He could have turned around and followed the brothers who had just left, but he decided against it. Now that they'd split up it was bootless to follow little parties up and down the country. Besides, if he kept showing up in their haunts they might notice him and remember him.

The barman asked questions.

"Are you with the party from Leiningen going to the river?"

"I'm going west."

He thought the barman might be in a position know some things. But how to ask?

"Perhaps a friend of mine came through here? I was given to understand he was traveling on this road. About my size; about my age. He bears a scar across his nose. A well-spoken man; a gentleman; a gallant. He would have been escorting a beautiful dark lady and her little maid. He wears a sword with a gold-chased pommel."

"I remember no such man."

"You would remember him if you had seen him."

"Perhaps I did not see him. Even innkeepers sleep."

"Perhaps he did not pass."

In time the messengers left. The drink was pleasant, but Conrad saw no use in remaining. He could return in the evening.

He rose, cast some coins on the bar, and left the inn. Rather than walk back up the street, he decided to loop around, outside the blockhouse. He passed the stamping stables where the horses rested and were readied for their next journey. In the yard between stable and blockhouse, a great beast was being shoed by a big man in an apron.

It was a fine bright day, not too warm, not too windy. A soft path led behind the town, if town it could be called, and toward the woodsman's cottage. The path stayed level, while the street and the town rose gradually on a ridge. Someone had built a low stone wall behind the shops and houses, and it rose with the ridge at a slow steady angle. Above the wall, Conrad could see the line of red roofs and the upper stories of the taller buildings.

At the street's end and highest point, Conrad saw the square tower of middle height, though now, with the added height of the slope supporting it, it looked like quite a respectable fortification. He could see the window with the white washing put out, and he stopped to watch it fluttering in the sun like a banner.

As he watched, he saw a bright-haired young woman lean out the window and begin pulling the washing in. Conrad now saw that the clothes were hanging from a line fixed on a long pole like a yardarm.

He started, then he stared, fixed in place. For the woman was Liese. Even at this distance, he could recognize her with no mistake. Liese here, and if Liese, then the Countess and Flik-Flak? He crouched down by instinct, close to the undergrowth bordering the path, and began moving rapidly toward the woodsman's cottage. When he passed beyond sight of the tower, he took off at a run.

He stopped at the door and composed himself, taking deep breaths, forcing himself to slow down. When he entered the house, he found the woodsman's wife seated by the window, at her sewing. She must have seen him running.

"Günther has arrived?"

"Not yet, not yet. The lady Proserpina, is she out?" he asked, using Peregrina's alias.

"No, no. Still in your room. I fear she is unwell."

Conrad walked through the heavy curtain that marked off the entrance to their guest room. There he found Peregrina lying on her back in bed, reading a small octavo volume with no great appearance of interest, holding it above her.

"You are unwell?" he asked.

"I am fine. You have news?"

"I have seen ..."

But she waved him to silence.

"Come outside. We will go for a walk in the woods. I do not trust this woodsman's wife."

AT WORK KUTTA ASKED him: "Are you stalking Charlotte?"

"I beg your pardon?"

"Charlotte. Are you stalking her?"

Kutta was smiling, but a little warily.

"Such a question."

"I heard you were in her neighborhood."

"Conrad goes where he wishes. I thought that was well known."

Kutta didn't know quite what to make of that.

Conrad was disappointed, not in Kutta so much as in Charlotte. But perhaps she only mentioned the encounter in passing.

It was all becoming very tiresome, this work. After festering quietly for years–a manageable discontent, no different from thousands upon thousands of other working lives–his displeasure had suddenly intensified, like some kind of Black Swan-triggered stock crash, and he found himself saddled by a heavy sour anger that he feared was not going away.

In a couple of weeks they'd debut the new "live" demo. If it went well, it could go on without him, and he would find it yet one degree more difficult to justify his usefulness to the company. If it did not go well, most of the blame would fall on him. The time was coming for a severance.

In the meantime, he had been working on his Action Document–the individual employee's humble contribution to the grand Strategic Planning Document–his vision for the future, the one bright spot in his working days. He felt sure he had come up with some ideas that management would find interesting.

"HA! LIESE. AND THE Countess and that wretch must be with her. What luck! We could have gone right past them and never known it."

Conrad and Peregrina were seated in a small clearing, both on a fallen tree of great girth. The floor of the clearing was cool and damp and dark green, while above, where the sun caught the tops of the trees, the leaves glittered a pale emerald. It was a peaceful scene, or would have been, were it not for Peregrina.

"Is it possible?" Conrad said. "Would Flik-Flak go to ground here, where the Brotherhood passes through every day, to say nothing of travelers and townsmen who might be only too happy to betray him?"

"It is just like Flik-Flak. Exactly like him. How he would laugh to think of the hunt passing through here, and all the time him sipping wine and playing at cards in the tower. A perfect audacity; one he would savor. No doubt he has a friend in the tower who would hide him. He has friends in many places, though one less than he did."

She considered for a few moments, then went on.

"But there is more to this tale. I see it now. This place is the emperor's waystation. The Eagle Messengers pass through here every day. Flik-Flak could play one against the other, the Eagle against the Raven. If the Brotherhood tried to take the lady away, the emperor's men would come to her aid. From the old days, a century ago and more, when a Mittelsbach used the ring to rescue the emperor from the dungeons of the sultan. They remember and would come to the aid of any Mittelsbach. Indeed, if the empire was what it once was, and if the emperor was what his grandfather was, they would be scouring the countryside now to find her, and the Baron of Reichenstein would never have dared to kidnap her in the first place. But things are not as they were. Men are not as they were."

She sighed.

"So, Flik-Flak drinks Spanish wine in a snug castle, and the Countess does not dare stir outside for fear of the Brotherhood. You see his cunning? Well, no more."

She stood with great decision and began marching rapidly toward the town.

"What do you intend?" asked Conrad.

"I will call him out of his castle. We were lucky to find them here. We may not be so lucky again."

"But, my lady, you must allow for the possibility ... There was something distinctly domestic about the scene I saw, with Liese taking in the washing. Is it not possible that Flik-Flak has succeeded in his aim, and he has married the lady already?"

"Never. I know something of these Mittelsbachs. She would never give in to pressure, not so easily, not so soon."

"Perhaps she did not have a choice?"

"A forced marriage?" They were now passing the woodsman's cottage. "Never. Even if he could find a churchman to perform it, a forced marriage is no marriage. That is God's law and man's. Such a marriage would be useless to Flik-Flak. He must come to possess the treasures honestly, by right, or they would be useless to him."

"Perhaps he has won her over."

"Ha!"

Peregrina increased her speed the closer she got to the town. She was gripping the hilt of her short broad bandit's sword.

"My lady, would not circumspection be advisable ...?"

She saw the tower and broke into a run, Conrad following behind.

She burst out onto the head of the street and ran to the base of the tower, taking her stand outside the courtyard.

She drew her sword.

"Flik-Flak," she cried. "We have found you! Come out and face the woman you wronged."

Conrad glanced quickly behind him and saw that Peregrina was already attracting interest.

"Show yourself," she cried.

For a long moment there was nothing, then Flik-Flak appeared in the window drying his hands with a towel.

"My lady Peregrina, it does my heart good to see you! You are looking well, and you too my new friend. I knew that they would not be able to hold you. This is a happy reunion."

"What are you saying? Do you dare? Come down here at once."

"I fear that, with circumstances as they are ... Perhaps it would be better if you came up to me."

Conrad saw that two of Flik-Flak's men, the very two who had steered the boat for him, had come out of the tower door and were lounging about in the courtyard. They were armed. He thought it prudent to draw his own sword.

"Dear Peregrina, surely you are not thinking to come to blows over such a little jest as I played on you by the river?"

"You think you can talk your way out of this you ... you ... Flik-Flak? Come down, I say."

A crowd was beginning to gather. Conrad heard them talking in excited whispers, "Flik-Flak! It is Flik-Flak!"

Flik-Flak, a name that had been bestowed on him for its fanciful resemblance to the swift drawing of his blade and its first cut. Surely Peregrina did not seriously consider facing him at crossed swords. Yet her reputation for audacity was scarcely less than his own.

There was a positive hubbub behind them as word of the brawl spread.

"Come down!"

"On the contrary, dear lady, I must insist that you come up. If you look behind you, you will see our mutual enemy, *die Schwarze Brudershaft*, coming hotfoot this way. It would go ill with either of us if we fell into their hands."

All heads turned. The crowd involuntarily shrank back, and sure enough, Conrad and Peregrina saw beyond them three Brothers of the Raven running up the hill, and beyond those, just passing the inn, still more mounted on great black horses. They were here in strength.

"Come my friends, join me in the tower. We can face them together, and settle our own little differences later. Come up!"

The two henchmen at the base stood back on either side of the open door. A moment's indecision, only that, and Peregrina raced for the tower.

Chapter 6

AT ELEVEN O'CLOCK OF a Thursday morning, Conrad once more stood before the door of Lady Diana's museum. Behind him the street life passed unheeded. He reached the sculpted doorknob and gave it a gentle twist. It did not budge. The door was locked. Could he have made a mistake?

He looked at the museum hours again where they were painted on the glass, and was surprised to see that most of the gold was gone; only the outlines of the letters and numbers remained, and in some places they were gone entirely.

He hesitated a moment, only a moment, and pressed the pearl doorbell. He heard an answering tone, somewhere in the recesses of the sealed building. He waited a while, then rang again. Perhaps she was out.

Then he was aware, before he could see anything, of a faint disturbance just inside the door. The curtain moved aside, and he saw a woman peering at him through the glass. He stepped back and waited with what he hoped was an encouragingly mild look on his face. He could see, even through the various reflections on the panes, that she was considering whether or not to open the door. At last he heard locks sliding back and ratcheting open; then the door swung back and the woman herself stepped into the opening.

"Can I help you?"

She was a woman of middle height, perhaps a little more, with straight dark hair and arresting dark eyes under fine dark brows, with a high white forehead and cheekbones both high and wide. A woman to be stared at; not old as Charlotte thought, younger than Conrad himself. She was formally attired in a long dress that rustled when she moved. Her bearing could only be described as regal. She had not the

71

slenderness of a young girl or of an older woman overgiven to stringent dieting, but had spread to an appropriate, still shapely, maturity.

"Yes? Can I help you?"

She was staring at Conrad with quite understandable suspicion, given the long siege she had been subjected to by her neighbors.

"I was hoping to view the museum."

"Oh. That. I'm sorry but I have closed the museum. It was too much trouble trying to keep up with the constant regulatory demands. Also, I began to fear for the collection. This museum and I, we have been subject to harassment, as you may know."

"Yes, I have heard. I am sorry. I understand. It is a disappointment though, I was hoping to see the collection. I've heard good things."

"Have you? I am glad."

"One of my coworkers, Charlotte, used to work for you I believe."

"Oh yes, Charlotte. You work with her? How is she?"

"Very well. We work at a place called Business Data Intercontinental a little north of here. My name is Conrad Kemper."

They shook hands. She seemed to relax, reassured now that he was not one of her tormenters.

"I am sorry you came out here for nothing." Then, impulsively, "Let me show you around. The collection is still where it was. It's a very small gallery."

He stepped inside.

He was almost struck blind for a moment by the change in light. The curtains were drawn and the large central room was unlit save for whatever sunlight managed to find a way around the edges. Lady Diana moved to the wall, popped a dimmer switch and eased it on about a quarter. Then she passed from one exhibit pillar to another, moving like Morticia Addams in her long rustling dress, and turned on the exhibition spotlights, one after another. When that was done, and Conrad's eyes had adjusted, she began the tour.

She began with the silver. All the old identifying tags were still mounted alongside the pieces. She proclaimed what was evidently a well-rehearsed museum spiel, enlivened by personal associations.

"This was the first piece great-grandpapa executed in the United States. It was never sold, but he kept it in the window of his shop as a show piece and sold several near copies. He never made an exact copy; it was against his philosophy. My parents kept this in their bedroom on top of the larger wardrobe. My mother kept flowers in it."

Conrad was enchanted. He stopped in front of a complex piece, a clouded glass goblet sitting on an intricately worked base in the form of an eagle, with a lid shaped as a woman's perfect torso, like a ship's figurehead.

"How old is this? Did your great grandfather do it? It seems ..."

The Lady was pleased.

"Yes, great-grandpapa worked more and more in an archaic style. Perhaps that is why his pieces sold so little in the latter part of his life. This is inspired by a sixteenth-century piece from Nürnberg. That was where he was from originally. As he became reconciled to dying in this country, he thought more and more about the old one. "

"So he was a *Nürnberger*."

"Yes, yes. You have a German name, where was your family from?"

"We were *Rheinländers* mostly. Mittelrhein."

"Oh, my mother's people were from the Middle Rhine. The Boppard area mostly."

"We still have family in Spay, just north of Boppard."

The costumes, all long dresses and complicated corseted ladies' undergarments, were not in fact the work of her great-grandmother. She had simply begun collecting them, inspired by her great-grandmother's legend, and now they formed the second part of the museum exhibit. They were stationed at odd places around the room, mounted on headless wasp-waisted full-bosomed frames of human size, and Conrad was repeatedly startled by them as he caught sight of one out of the corner of his eye or rounded a corner and found himself facing another.

It was a pleasant tour, one that the guide enjoyed as much as the guided, and when Conrad left in the early afternoon, he left with a dinner engagement for the following week.

CONRAD WAS IN A DARK room, a spacious dark room, with a lot of other people. There was commotion, a sense of urgency. The only light came from slit windows or leaked through from above, from the stairwell and a couple of apertures in the ceiling. He waited while his eyes became accustomed to the dimness.

Flik-Flak came partway down the stairs and stuck his head into the room.

"Welcome," he said. "This is an unexpected pleasure. It would be best, I think, if we most of us came upstairs where the windows are. Jürgen, stay down here by the door. Liese *schatz* perhaps you too could stay by the stove and boil us up some water. Put a little oil in it. The rest of you ..."

Soon they were all standing on the second floor, which seemed positively brilliant with sunlight. They could hear the growing hubbub outside. Flik-Flak strolled to the front window and leaned out to address the people.

"Gentlemen, and ladies, you make a brave gathering on so fine a day. But what are you all here for? What would you of Flik-Flak?"

"Send out the lady of Mittelsbach!" cried a voice.

"And come out yourself!" added another.

"Really, is this how you come to court a lady? I had hoped better of you. But I know I am on solid ground when I say that the Gräfin wants nothing to do with the Black Brotherhood, so my best advice to you is to go back the way you came and tell your master you were unable to find us."

"Come down and join us and you will see how soon we end your japes."

"A new verse to an old song," Flik-Flak observed.

He suddenly leaped back, laughing, followed almost immediately by an arrow that skittered off the ceiling and against the opposite wall.

"Seven and counting," he said. "It looks like some of the townsmen are throwing in with them as well. It will be a hard fight.

"So, La Peregrina, will you fight alongside us? I see you have Elvenbright by your side."

"You have the effrontery to ask me for help?"

"My lady," he said reproachfully. "A nice critic might judge that you have requited any slight wrong I may have done you by betraying our presence here and bringing our enemies upon us. The same critic might further judge that I have atoned for my offense by opening the door to the tower and saving you and your companion from the Ravens. Also, to urge a mere practical point, if we are overcome and the Black Knights take the tower, it will go hard with you. They blame you, with some justice, for rescuing the Gräfin. So come, my lady, let bygones be bygones. Together again?"

Peregrina did not answer, but scowled and went to sit by the fire, across from, as Conrad then noticed, the Countess of Mittelsbach, the ultimate object of everyone's interest.

Flik-Flak appraised Conrad.

"My friend ... Is it necessary that I ask?"

"Not necessary," said Conrad with a laugh. "I fight with Flik-Flak unless Peregrina gainsays. We have been companions on a long hunt, and I would not wish to go against her."

They looked towards Peregrina but she was speaking to the Countess.

"My lady, are you well?" she asked.

"Well enough," said the Countess. "If the next hour does not bring a change for the worse. But I thought to be safe back in my castle long before this. This is not what I expected when I left the baron's castle with you."

"Nor I. Flik-Flak is full of surprises."

Conrad approached the two women.

"Countess, I am overjoyed to see you again looking so well. I'm sorry that our affairs have followed the course that they have. The Lady Peregrina and I had other hopes. For now, I must say that I agree with Flik-Flak's judgment. We must all be friends again. It is for us to pick up the thread we dropped back at the river, so long ago or so it seems."

"Before Flik-Flak's treachery," said Peregrina.

"Just so."

Peregrina sniffed in contempt but raised no objection.

The Countess said, "It seems I have no choice but again to follow the course that necessity sets. I do not wish to fall into the hands of the Brotherhood; still less do I wish to come into the power of their black master."

Conrad turned back to his restored comrade.

"Should we not meet them downstairs?"

"We should not. I've had some opportunity to review the defensive arrangement of this tower. There are two doors, the greater door you came in by and a smaller door by the kitchen. Both are of stout oak reinforced with iron and scarcely less impregnable than the wall itself. It would be some time before they could force an entry that way. The windows are too narrow to admit a person. No, the assault will come from above, through the great window and the open roof. Jürgen can watch below. The rest of us must prepare a defense."

They walked together and looked out the front window at the gathering crowd.

"It is a pity we haven't any bow," Flik-Flak said. "The master of this tower was no hunter."

"What about the townsmen? There are many outside. What side do you think they will take?"

"Alas, I fear the townsmen are moved by a spirit of commerce not honor or adventure. They will not go against the Ravens who come to this town and stop at their inn every day and shop in their stores. Some may even help them."

"It seems a poor outlook," Conrad said. "In the long run. If they gather any strength at all there is little hope of escape."

"We have a few cards in our hand. First, they won't do anything to endanger their prize, the Gräfin. Second, the Messenger Knights of the Eagle come too to this town. When they learn what is afoot they are sure to come in on the side of Mittelsbach. There is a history between Mittelsbach and the empire as you may know. They would join in, I think, just for a chance to fight the Ravens, and they too have friends among the townsfolk. So 'Hold fast and trust in the Eagles'—let that be our watchword."

"A good plan. Yet if they do drive off the Black Brotherhood and rescue our Countess, it may go hard with Flik-Flak."

"Perhaps. But he will still be the one who rescued the Gräfin of Mittelsbach from the Ravens. And I have offered no insult to the lady while she was in my care. No, we will make a fine stand here, and Flik-Flak's spirits are still high."

"Are they ever otherwise?"

"I cannot recall."

They prepared. They gathered missiles at the foot of the wide main window. There were loose bricks in the hearth which they prized free and lined up. Flik-Flak sent Stefan, his second henchman, to the open roof with orders to gather slates and debris. There was an old spear suspended over the hearth, which Flik-Flak took down and set Peregrina to wrapping and widening its end, with a view toward creating an implement that could be used to push a ladder away from the tower. All the while the noise outside grew louder.

Flik-Flak stepped lightly to the window and looked out.

"Ten now," he said. "We are unlucky. Joined by some of the bolder town folk."

He slipped to the side of the opening just before another arrow passed inside.

"This could become an inconvenience," he said.

"The table?" suggested Conrad.

They dragged the heavy plank table across the floor and propped it up in front of the window. Now it was possible to peak around the sides in less danger.

A loud blow resounded against the door downstairs, followed by a cry from Liese.

"They are trying to break the door below," said Flik-Flak. "I have seen their axe, a light affair for chopping sticks. It must be the townsmen; the Ravens would know better." He called downstairs, "Fear not Liese, the door is proof. In fact, you had better take the water off the boil for a while, so it does not all waste away."

The hatchet blows on the door soon stopped. The crowd noise continued, but was followed by no general assault.

"Now, I think, some refreshment."

Flik-Flak produced a bottle from a small standing cupboard and twisted the cork free in a practiced motion. After the brandy had passed from hand to hand, he said, "I must go and see to Stefan," and rose up the winding stair, with the bottleneck firmly in hand.

"I wonder why the delay," said Conrad.

"Gathering strength, I expect," said Peregrina.

"They are lashing together ladders," said the Countess. She had moved to the window and was studying the scene with a sporting interest, with her face set close to the table's edge. "They have many short ladders and they are cobbling together longer ones."

"My lady," cried Conrad in alarm. "Please come away from the window. A stray arrow might find its way through. They cannot see from below who is looking at them."

She suffered herself to be led away from the dangerous gap, not without a wry smile on her face.

"My genie is protecting me once more."

Flik-Flak came jauntily down the stairs with the bottle held in one hand and an arrow in the other.

"Snatched out of the air," he said. "It was a brilliant feat. It is true the arrow lost velocity with the altitude, but still ... Who but Flik-Flak?"

He continued down to bring brandy and cheer to the first story.

Arrows continued at long intervals to sail over the table or stick into it. Flik-Flak returned and they all moved out of the line of fire and sat on the floor. Still, none of them could resist looking out from time to time despite the danger.

"A dozen now. They gather like flies. Ach, I see they are bringing a much stouter axe."

"Where? Let me see?"

Peregrina sprang up and shouldered Flik-Flak aside.

"That woodsman! It is his axe, I am sure. Yet he did not come himself. Didn't I tell you?" she looked at Conrad.

Flik-Flak grasped her by her sturdy upper arms and gently moved her aside, resuming his place.

"The ladders are moving! Friends, let us prepare to receive our guests." He called down, "Liese put the water on the boil."

The pace of the archery suddenly increased and one of the missiles forced its metal tip through the wood. The shouts outside grew louder, and a new, heavier axe blow struck the door downstairs.

Then they heard Stefan calling from the roof: "The Eagles! The Eagles are coming."

"I WASN'T HAPPY WITH it," Kutta said.

"Were there technical problems?" asked Herrick.

They were sitting, the three of them–Kutta, Conrad and Herrick–in the second conference room. It was an informal meeting. They had taken to hanging around together, the three old hands, and it was natural for them to run over the latest demo, among other things.

"No, it worked fine. The demonstration just kept getting sidetracked. It was less easy ... I didn't control the flow like I usually do. I don't think I was able to show everything the database can do."

"Would it help to expand the demo base?"

"That would make things worse. When it's a live demo, I've found they tend to fixate on pet problems that are only a small part of the big picture. We'll spend half an hour on one tiny little question."

"Still, if the customers are asking about what's important to them, isn't that all to the good?"

"The customers don't know what's important to them," Kutta said, but then he laughed. "It's a balance," he added. "I'll have to find it but I haven't found it yet."

"That'll come with time. Practice makes perfect."

"If I'm still around," Kutta replied and they were back on their familiar topic.

"You're safe," said Herrick.

"No one's safe," said Kutta. "It's a fourth-generation world, baby!"

"Have you guys been working on your Action Documents?" asked Herrick.

"Haven't done a thing with it."

"Assiduously," said Conrad.

"Seriously?" Herrick laughed. "You know, I'm your Team Leader. You have to submit your Action Document to me."

"Expect to be astonished."

They laughed.

"Strange times," said Herrick. "Strange times."

THERE WAS A PITCHED battle outside. The Ravens and Eagles were still arriving, and neither was giving an inch. They must have been sending out for reinforcements all around the countryside. The townsmen, all but the maddest spirits, had pulled out of the debacle and were sheltering in their homes.

Three times the Ravens had tried to force an entry to the tower, through the window and over the roof. The implement Peregrina had fashioned for pushing over the ladder had failed in its task. It was not long enough to operate safely without the operator being exposed to arrows. The most they could do was push the ladder toward vertical, but the knights on the ground kept it steady. So they had taken off the padding and used the spear as a weapon, skewering one of the assailants. When he fell, he had taken the spear with him.

The bricks and missiles were all thrown, the oil-and-water spent. Stefan on the roof was dead, but they'd closed the trap door and the black knights could not batter their way through. On the last assault, several had made it into the room, and Flik-Flak and Conrad had had to beat them back with their swords.

The next determined assault was likely to succeed, if any there came. The Ravens were heavily occupied now with their imperial enemies, and it was not impossible that the tower would be forgotten.

Flik-Flak watched from the window, behind the pin-cushion table which had been propped up for the fifth or sixth time.

"Open warfare between the black and the gold," he said contentedly. "This bodes ill for the country. It was a long time brewing."

"What now?" Peregrina stood beside him.

"Now we wait for our chance."

Jürgen came up the stairs, just a moment after the smell of smoke reached them.

"They have fired both doors and the lower story. The timbers in the wall have caught. Soon it will be running through the floor."

"I thought you said they wouldn't do that!" Liese said. "That they wouldn't endanger the lady."

"An act of anger and despair," said Flik-Flak. "Their mood has changed. They must feel the battle slipping away."

Then to Jürgen, "Can they come through the door? I must see."

They ran down the stairs and only a few moments later came running back up.

"The fire is spreading too fast. They will not come in, but we can't go out."

He ran to the window and cast aside the table.

"They've left the ladder. We can go down as they came up."

"Madness!" said Peregrina.

"The arrows!" said Liese. "We can't."

"Would you rather burn?"

The smoke was coming thick up the stairs and spreading across the ceiling.

"We will assist you," said Flik-Flak. "Fear not, they will not shoot at the ladies. They may not shoot at any of us; the fire may have been their parting shot."

He peered out the window.

"Now. They are occupied. Conrad, my friend, may I lay the duty on you to lead the way? My lady Gräfin, follow close behind. Then Peregrina and Liese close together, moving as one. Jürgen and I will assist you over the balcony."

"Ooooh," Liese was screwing up her courage, but she would go when the word was given.

Flik-Flak cast his eye one last time around the tower that had been his dwelling.

"A lovely tower," he muttered. "A proper home. Such a shame to see it burn."

Conrad went to the window, and stepped over the sill onto a half-balcony. Already it was night outside. He gave a quick glance over the battlefield, enough to see that he was not at the moment targeted, and took a long step onto the ladder.

He descended a few rungs and watched as the Countess was helped over. Now that he was outside he could see smoke sliding from the window and was conscious of the roaring of the flames. They had set the roof ablaze as well. It was a difficult judgment whether to shield the Countess with his body or to leave space so that their enemies could see her clearly and spare her if they had a mind to. He decided against trusting to the mercy of the Ravens, now that the battle had gone against them. He waited until she was on the ladder and descended step for step with her, with his upper body covering her lower, and his arms framing her on the ladder in a protective embrace.

When they reached the bottom, they held the ladder, one on each side.

Peregrina followed, and Liese, only hesitating a moment, both conducted by Jürgen and Flik-Flak. At the bottom they all stood and looked up, fascinated by the spectacle in spite of themselves.

Now it was Flik-Flak's turn. He swung easily onto the ladder, and instead of stepping down he grabbed the sides, placed his feet on the outside, and simply slid down. When he hit ground he looked up, in time to see Jürgen at the top of the ladder take an arrow through the back and slump over the balcony. Their luck had run out, and a vindictive Raven had noticed their exodus and acted.

"He is struck!" cried Peregrina.

"He is killed. He will not survive that," said Flik-Flak. He hesitated a moment, then said. "I can do nothing for Stefan, but I will not leave Jürgen to be burned."

He clambered up the ladder and back into the room, where he could be seen in the window, hoisting Jürgen on his back and draping both of his comrade's arms over his shoulders. He pinioned Jürgen's arms in place with his own left arm and somehow, using his right arm to hold himself steady on the ladder, he swung his legs over the balcony and began his descent.

"Flik-Flak." Peregrina spoke one word in admiration.

He moved down slowly now. Twice the man on his back was stuck by bolts, but nothing carried through to Flik-Flak.

When he reached bottom and laid the now dead Jürgen on the ground, Flik-Flak said, "Even in death he protects his master." Then to the others, "You waited for us. It was handsomely done."

They felt the heat from the tower. On that side all was light, but in the rest of the town night had fallen and the battle had become a confused struggle of silhouettes.

"Jürgen can rest where he is. The fire will not touch him here. The rest of us must get to the Eagles' lines." He pointed. "All together. Let us surround the Gräfin and let her name be our battle cry, so they know our party."

They sprinted through the dark, under the rising smoke and falling embers, toward the line of the Knight-Messengers of the Empire, and as they ran they called out, "Mittelsbach! Mittelsbach!"

Chapter 7

SHE WAS A RESPECTABLE trencherwoman. She stayed the course through dessert and coffee. Her name, it turned out, was Lindt, like the chocolatier. He resisted easy jokes.

She wasn't quite dressed in one of the magnificent creations that graced her museum, but there was a definite archaic quality to her garb: an embroidered vest somewhat reminiscent of a corset, a fairly long skirt. White poofy sleeves. Conrad didn't know the terms. She had certain old lady qualities centered in the deliberation of her movements and formality of her speech, and certain little girl qualities in the guileless way she spoke her mind and in her direct questions and frank admission of ignorance. Conrad began to feel she might be ridiculous in the same way that he was.

They discussed houses.

"I don't know if I helped myself or hurt myself by closing the museum," she said. "They won't be able to trouble me about lack of access or sprinklers or any of that folderol. On the other hand maybe it's easier for them to force a private house to move by eminent domain. Do you know?" and she blinked her great dark eyes across the table at him.

"I don't," said Conrad, who also had no problem admitting ignorance. "It seems a strange area of law. Lawlessness, really, might over right. I imagine the judgments are very *ad hoc*, and susceptible to pressure from outside. And inducements. I suppose I am being discouraging."

"I'm already discouraged. But it's my house! Why should I not be allowed to live at peace in my own home? And why should these people be permitted to harass me? The police have been sweet, the ones I have spoken to, but they will only act after some outrage has already been committed."

"Can't a judge issue some kind of restraining order?"

"They have the right to protest, so they say." She stopped to take a sip. "Do you know most of the protesters, the ones who want me out, are from the Criminal Justice department? Ha! That and Urban Studies. When my house was built, there was no Municipal University campus here. There was no Municipal University."

Conrad commiserated.

"The whole thing seems absurd. They've just got the money to keep it going."

"And I don't. I suppose I could get a lot of money for selling. But I love my old house. I grew up there. It's really the only thing keeping me here. I suppose that sounds silly."

"Not to me, not at all. I don't live in a museum like you, but I feel the same way ... in a similar way about my own house. It's where I grew up. It holds the memories of my parents and grandparents."

He told her about the architectural drawings on the walls, the pictures of old Germany, of places he'd never been, places gone forever, of his mother's paintings and his mother's paints.

"It's the only thing holding me here too, in New York. Outside, everything has changed. Everyone we knew has moved away or died. It's like a fortress. But it's not under siege."

She understood. She ordered apple cobbler for dessert because it was the closest thing to strudel. She did not ask him about work once. Conrad began to think he had really found something here.

CONRAD WAS SEATED ON a blanket, close to the eaves of a forest. There were tents pitched to his right and left, and people constantly arriving and going away. From where he sat he could see the woodsman's cottage.

He was sitting with the Countess of Mittelsbach, and they were in the camp of the Eagles. The smell of last night's burning hung in the air.

They heard snatches of the Eagles' talk.

"The town is swept clear. No Ravens to be seen for miles."

"It was time they be taught a lesson. Past time."

"The townsmen too. They have forgotten this is our outpost, an imperial outpost not a den of robbers. They must be taught. They must be reminded."

"I cannot stay. I must return to the *Hauptstadt* at once with urgent news. I am already late."

"A difficult situation," said one, who appeared to be an officer of some kind, a bit older than the others, a bit more cured by wind and weather. "We all have our missions which need to be completed. But we must first secure the town."

"Perhaps we can send the messengers out one by one."

"What I was thinking. A risk, though, a distinct risk, what with the Ravens on the warpath. And then there is the Countess ..." and he looked down where Conrad and the lady were seated.

"My lady."

He looked down on her, then felt something disrespectful in his posture and took a seat on the blanket.

"Where is it that you wish to go?"

"My preference is to return to my home, to Schloss Mittelsbach, by the shortest road."

"Have you an escort?"

"I have my faithful Conrad."

Conrad bowed in place.

"That is good. But the Ravens are running mad across the country. I would like to send others with you if they can be spared."

"That is kind of you, Captain Eckhard. But I heard you talking and understand you are under some pressure. If it proves necessary I can certainly wait until you have your affairs in order."

"That is most gracious. I will take the roll call here and in town and see where we stand. We lost too many good men and some are *hors de combat*. I will return later in the afternoon."

After Captain Eckhard had left, Conrad leaned toward the Countess and asked a question that had been troubling him some time.

"Flik-Flak. Where is he?"

"I don't know. I have been looking."

"I haven't seen Peregrina either."

"Nor I. Look, here is Liese; perhaps she has heard."

Liese threaded her way through the golden knights, laden with bread, cheese and bottles, looking pink but pleased at the appreciative comments directed at her by the crossing gallants. She deposited her cargo on the blanket and sat down beside it.

"Liese, dear," said her mistress. "We were just wondering what has become of Flik-Flak. Have you seen him?"

"No, my lady. He's no longer in town. He left shortly after he brought us through the lines to safety."

"Ah," the Countess nodded.

"And Peregrina," said Conrad. "I have not seen her either."

Liese ducked her head and spoke to the ground.

"Peregrina left with him. With Flik-Flak. I saw her go."

"Did she so?" Conrad laughed. "After all that happened? Did she so?"

He laughed again and set to opening the cheese wheel.

"The heart of a woman," said the Countess sagely. "Who can understand it?"

"Men have hearts too," said Liese shyly.

"Do they? I have not observed it," said the Countess, but then she laughed, and she and Conrad laughed together.

"CONRAD! HEY, CONRAD."

An urgent whisper. They stopped him as he passed Herrick's office. Kutta was already standing inside. Herrick was seated at his desk. It was a big desk in a small office. The walls were covered with cork boards, the boards with papers and drawings and charts.

"Have you heard any of this talk about product lines being dropped?"

"I did not. Is that the rumor now?"

"It's going around. I tried to sound out Lydia, but I got nothing. Less than nothing. She got snippy with me."

"She's been in a bad mood lately," said Herrick.

"She must have heard about you stalking Charlotte," said Kutta. "Jealous."

The joke was getting old.

"Perhaps it is the strain of dating Lagonigro," Conrad suggested. "These finance men are by nature ill-suited to gallantry. Their work bleeds over into personal selfishness."

"If you say so."

"It's a bad sign," Herrick said. "If it's true. Cutting product lines. I've seen it before. You know what it makes me think?"

They obliged him with expectant looks.

He gave a quick glance around, though there was no one but the three of them in the office.

"Acquisition. It makes me think we're being acquired and they're making moves to smooth the process."

"Uh-huh," said Kutta. "I didn't want to say."

Then after a pause, he said, "So. Have either of you started looking?"

"Not actively," said Herrick. "But I'm aware. Ear to the ground, that sort of thing."

"I've started looking," said Kutta. "You?"

"No," said Conrad.

"You must be confident."

"Not confident. I just don't care."

"I THOUGHT THE STORY was well-known. But of course you are a stranger here."

"I have heard it in part from Peregrina. I don't know how well she knows it."

"Yes, tales change with time and many tellings. And perhaps only a Mittelsbach can tell it truly. It was this way ..."

They were sitting on the grass in a forest clearing. They had stopped for a late afternoon supper, rabbit stew with herbs. The golden light of the afternoon was reflected in the golden leaves of the trees above them. Now and again, single leaves fell from above, spiraling down and coming to ground with a light tap. Autumn was stealing upon them.

The knights who were breaking down the cooking pot and tripod and kicking dirt over the fire, preparing to strike camp, paused in their labors and leaned towards the lady.

"My many times great-grandfather, Carolus, the first Count of Mittelsbach, was a huntsman of some renown. He was a simple knight by birth, of no particular property and of no special position, and he lived at the edge of the great wood which covered all the lands around Mittelsbach at the time. One could ride for days in the trackless wilderness and never meet another human soul, and it was there that Carolus was happiest. There came a day when Sir Carolus in his wanderings crossed a ridge that was just one ridge farther than any he had ever been, and upon descending into a narrow dark valley, he started a beautiful white hind such as he had never seen before. You have noticed that the white hind is the emblem of my family? It is from this hind that our fortune sprang, long ago.

"Sir Carolus loosed his two good hounds against it and rode after them. For a long time he followed the belling of the hounds, far from his own familiar lands, far and farther, so that, woodsman though he was, in the end even he could not guess the way back. At the last, the sound of the hounds faded away. He stopped on his sweating and blowing horse for a long time listening, listening, but he never heard those hounds again nor found the white hind.

"He dismounted and tried to follow the trail on foot. For a while he tracked them in the soft earth of the forest floor, but in the end the trail was lost over the rocks of the mountainside. As night was coming on, Sir Carolus began to look for a place to stop. Just when he thought the site most deserted, he heard voices, men speaking, and he followed the sound through the darkening trees. And lo! in a clearing watered by a quiet stream, he saw, by the side of a well-built fire, trussed up like game for the spit, a bearded dwarf such as used to inhabit those places in the long ago before men came. There were two men standing over him, if men they were, more like half-trolls, the survivings of the uncouth tribe that left their stone monuments all over these lands.

"Though the dwarf was an unlovely creature, it went against Sir Carolus' heart to see the two pitiless miscreants standing over him, promising him torments or worse while he writhed helpless against his bonds. We Mittelsbachs have always been known as soft-hearted.

'What do you mean to do with that dwarf?' he asked.

'What is it to you? We have business with him.'

'It offends me to see a fellow creature so treated.'

'Be off or you'll join him.'

"That was enough provocation for my many times great-grandfather. He drew his short hunting sword, though he was already weary from his long hunt. It was a hard fight, for though Sir Carolus was accounted highly as a swordsman and the ruffians were no better armed than he, or maybe a little bit worse, there were two of them and they were strong and active. In the end, he prevailed and slew them both, though he was sore hurt in the struggle.

"As he bent over the dwarf and released him from his bonds, he cursed himself as a fool for the trouble taken over what seemed now but a sorry creature. For a while the dwarf sat chafing his wrists and ankles where the rope had bitten him and grumbling to himself, while Sir Carolus looked down upon him.

"But of a sudden, the dwarf sprang to his feet and drew himself up. Then no longer did he seem a pitiable creature, but a man of worth.

'I am Nargrim of Erdheim, and I am a king and the son of a king. My people are scattered and my kingdom is gone, but a king is a king forever. For what you have done in rescuing me from those two churls, you will receive a gift that only a dwarf king can give. Those fools were only after my gold such as they believe all dwarves to hold. But you I will give three gifts beyond price, gifts that no other man on earth has the like of, to serve you and your heirs.'

"Then he recited this verse:

> *Three times three from the dwarf king's hall*
> *Three times three for to win, know and call*
> *An heirloom for Mittelsbachs yet unborn*
> *Silk banner, silver ring and gold-trimmed horn*

"He raised his staff from the ground where it had been dropped by the churls, and brought it down to earth, striking with the metal tip.

"As soon as staff struck ground there was a flash, and lo! they were standing in a vast hall, that seemed to Sir Carolus to be fashioned by skill from a great mountain cave. The ceiling was impossibly high, the walls shone with many colors, a fountain ran and bubbled in the center of the hall and fed a stream that flowed across the floor through a dwarf-wrought channel and out the great open doorway. The pillars were carved into the likenesses of trees, a canopied throne sat empty upon a marble stair, and everywhere Sir Carolus looked there was something to delight the eye and amaze the mind. Indeed, it is said that the great hall of Schloss Mittelsbach was designed to follow my many times great-grandfather's memory of this magical hall. And yet, there were no gentle-dwarves or servants to people the hall, and no queen, only the king Nargrim and Sir Carolus himself.

"It was there that the dwarf king gave Sir Carolus his reward, the three treasures, and explained the uses of each one. A red silken banner, and when it is carried into battle, no matter the odds, the cause of the banner would prevail. A silver ring, and the wearer of it would know the secret thoughts of others. A gold-trimmed horn, made from some great beast long passed from the earth, and the one who blew it would summon help from another world. Three gifts of wonder, and each could be used only three times, after which their power would sleep silent forever.

"After he had given him the gifts, Nargrim said, 'Never forget, never let your family forget, that it was I Nargrim, a forgotten king from a forgotten race, who bestowed these marvels upon you. Let the story be told as long as the Mittelsbachs endure.'

"And he struck the polished floor of the mountain hall, and in a second flash like the first, my many times great-grandfather Carolus found himself once again in the forest, with the fire burnt out, the two churls still lying, and his horse wandered away. But he held the three treasures and we hold them still."

All stayed silent a long time, considering what they'd heard. Conrad spoke first, as much to break the spell as to find the answer to his question.

"I have heard that the banner had been used once already before the dwarf king gave it to the Mittelsbachs."

"That is incorrect," said the Countess. "What happened is that Sir Carolus was forced to use the banner himself before he won his way back to his home. It was a long hard trip, fraught with danger and adventure. But that, as they say, is another story."

A notion rose to the surface to Conrad's mind.

"My lady, where are those gifts now?"

"Safe at Castle Mittelsbach, of course."

Conrad sprang to his feet.

"My lady, we must hurry. Flik-Flak has gone there to steal them, I am sure of it."

The lady rose, and Conrad could see the same certainty dawning on her.

"But why?" Liese objected. "What good would they do him? They work for none but a Mittelsbach, I have heard that many times."

"Why?" cried Conrad. "For the outrage ... for the deed."

"He is Flik-Flak," said one of the knights, as if reciting a proverb. "No explanation is necessary, no explanation is sufficient."

"I have heard it said he never abandons an enterprise unless a greater one presents itself," said the lady. "Yes, he is going for the treasures."

"He has the start on us, a day at least. We must ride!"

"IS THAT KUTTA?"

Charlotte had stopped outside Conrad's office.

"It sounds like him," said Conrad.

Someone was raging in the distance. It was Kutta's voice, but in an unaccustomed register, used in an unaccustomed way. Conrad and Charlotte listened for a while.

"Do you know what's wrong?" she asked.

"Not specifically. I can make a guess."

He rose and passed into the open general office space. He was interested.

He found Kutta alone in his office, already having passed the peak of vocalized anger. He was valuable, and mercurial, enough that Conrad expected management would allow him his outburst without intervening.

Conrad poked his head in the doorway.

"Something wrong?" he asked.

"Conrad. Did you hear about Econstar Academy? They're cancelling it."

Conrad whistled.

"Really? Wow." He was finding it hard to match Kutta's emotion. "Where did you hear that?"

"From Noakes. Straight from the horse's ass. What am I supposed to tell the people I sold the damn thing to?"

"Aren't they going to keep supporting it?"

"Yeah, for a while. They say. 'For the duration of the contract.' But you know how it is. If they're not invested in it ..."

"Did they say why?"

"Vague stuff. Going in a different direction. You know. I'm surprised you're not pissed. You put a lot into it."

Conrad tried to muster indignation, out of courtesy to Kutta if nothing else, but failed.

"I guess I've been expecting changes. And if it's part of the whole acquisition situation, there's no sense getting mad at Noakes. Who knows how secure his job is?"

"Yeah. *If* we're being acquired. Which we still don't know for sure."

Kutta considered.

"It makes sense though. It would explain a lot."

He considered some more.

"Do you think they'll offer severance?"

CONRAD COULDN'T REMEMBER what one did. Especially now that they were no longer young. Where does one go? Fortunately, she seemed tractable and her interests aligned with his.

He took her to The Cloisters, a fairly easy ride from Yonkers. They walked the halls and gardens at a stately pace. They lingered in the Boppard gallery.

"Those are from the Karmaliterkirche," said Conrad, as they stood before the stained glass windows.

"I wonder how they got here," said Diana Lindt.

"I wonder how this whole place got here," said Conrad, looking around.

She knew many technical details, how things were made, not just the silver—of which there was a great deal—but also the carvings, glass and tapestries.

After they were finished they went down to Fort Tryon Park and picnicked on the grass. They sat on a checked blanket, one of Conrad's old table cloths. As always, Conrad took the time to appreciate the way her admirable bottom spread to its seat. Far away people played music on the radio. They poured chilled wine from a foil-wrapped bottle into plastic cups.

"It's very pleasant here," she said. "I haven't been here for many years."

"It's crowded," said Conrad. "More crowded than I remember."

"Everything is. I remember running on the grass when I was a little girl. There were no radios then. I mean no radios in the park. They had, of course, been invented."

She ate heartily. Despite her formal attire and diction, she struck Conrad as a woman of no pretense. She did not conceal or protect her emotions.

"It's remarkable," she said. "New York had come to seem very cold and alien to me. Very unfriendly. Especially with the troubles I've been having with the students and protestors. I didn't see anything but to become more and more isolated as I grew older. And now to meet a man like you. Most remarkable."

They tapped glasses while Conrad thought, "A man like me. But what am I like?"

Still, it was very pleasant to hear.

"ANOTHER HARD RIDE," said Liese.

Conrad, the Countess of Mittelsbach, and Liese were seated together on a low wooden bench outside another relay-station inn. They were waiting to change horses at one of the Eagle Messengers' staging places, another Wand'rerstand. The knights had decided this was the best way to catch up with Flik-Flak, to change horses on the way, and they had generously agreed to provide steeds from the emperor's own stock. Nothing too good for Mittelsbach. The three travelers were waiting while the grooms prepared their fresh mounts.

Conrad considered Liese. She seemed quite happy, despite her often vocally expressed fears. Conrad thought it would be difficult for her to go back to the stationary life of a serving girl when all this was over.

He addressed the Countess.

"I had a question, my lady, about the tale you told us, about the three treasures. If it is true that Sir Carolus used the banner to get home, and if it is also true, as I have heard, that another of the Mittelsbachs used it for his own purposes, does that mean there is yet one use left?"

"That is correct. A single certain victory for the one who uses it with right. Many a one would give a kingdom for it in the hope of winning a greater."

"And the ring has been used once?"

"Again correct. My three times grandfather Dietrich was forced to put the ring on his finger when it became necessary to rescue the Emperor Heinrich himself. The emperor had been captured, as you know, by the sultan's forces in the Little Kingdom when they were fighting there. They were planning to move the emperor down to the Sultanate, where it would be well-nigh impossible to rescue him. It was only by using the ring so that he could read the others' purposes that Grandfather Dietrich was able to circumvent them."

"A question, my lady," Liese piped up. "Why could he not leave the ring on? Then he would have the advantage of reading thoughts for the rest of his life."

The Countess shook her head gravely.

"No one could bear it. Scarcely was Grandfather Dietrich able to bear the little time he wore it. The constant din of others' thoughts clamoring for attention, driving out your own. He said he thought he would go mad. It was only duty that kept him to his task. Too, it does not do to hear the secret thoughts of your friends and lovers. You would soon have none. It was said that Grandfather Dietrich never fully trusted a soul after that. It is most unfortunate. And unjust. People's thoughts are so seldom at their own command. He knew it was unfair but he could never trust again; and he was afraid he could never love anyone whose thoughts he had heard. It was fortunate that he was far away from home at the time. No, the ring is best left alone."

"So," said Conrad after a pause. "The banner used twice and the ring once. And the horn never."

"The horn has been used once also," the Countess said.

"Has it? I did not know that. When?"

She looked at him and smiled.

"When I called you."

Chapter 8

"ARE YOU SURE YOU WANT to submit this?" Herrick asked.

They were sitting in Herrick's office. There wasn't a lot of space, either on the floor or on the walls or on the big desk. The stacks of papers and design paraphernalia, even in the digital age, claimed the lion's share.

"Sure. Why not?"

"How do you think management will take it?"

Good old Herrick. Blessed are the peacemakers.

"I stand behind my judgments. I've given my reasons."

"Yeah. No shortage of reasons. It just seems ... impolitic."

"I have never been politic."

"Less and less it seems."

Herrick furrowed his brow.

"Well it's your document," he said.

"My Action Document."

Herrick obliged with a little laugh.

"Right. Your Action Document. And you did say I'd be astonished."

"Are you?"

"I am."

"Then my work is done."

Herrick stood up.

"Well ..."

They shook hands, leaning across Herrick's desk. It felt like a final act. It felt like goodbye.

HE SAT IN THE DRAWING room listening to her play.

She played a little upright piano, almost a spinet. It was flawlessly polished but a little out of tune. She was well practiced; sometimes she propped up crumbling sheets of music against a hinged stand, sometimes she played by heart. He thought of her playing away the long evenings, to an audience of ghostly frames and empty dresses.

She played Mozart and Schubert, and folk tunes that were familiar to Conrad. Outside the common life of Yonkers carried on unheeding.

She sang.

> *Es zog ein Regiment*
> *Vom Ungarland herauf*
> *Es zog ein Regiment*
> *Vom Ungarland herauf*
> *Ein Regiment zu Fuß,*
> *Ein Regiment zu Pferd*
> *Ein Bataillon Deutschmeister*

He laughed with pleasure.

"Ah, I remember that one. My grandmother used to sing it."

"Come over and sing with me," said Diana Lindt. "We have the words here."

"Oh, I'm afraid I am not a singer."

"I can't believe that."

"It's true."

"Well ... no one's perfect, I suppose."

Conrad begged to differ.

THEY WERE IN MITTELSBACH country. A land of low wooded hills and green grass valleys. For miles now, the people by the side of the road had recognized the Countess and they doffed their hats and bowed. As they got closer to the castle, people waved and cheered. Children danced with excitement.

They had planned to ride straight on to the castle in hopes of getting there before Flik-Flak or of surprising him at his work. It became clear that they would have to stop for the sake of the horses.

"If we must, we must," said the Countess. "Let things fall out as they may."

They stopped outside a pleasant-looking inn with a conical roof and tables set outside. The Countess stayed at a distance and sent Liese inside with some of the knights. She sat on the grass alongside a clear, swift-flowing stream, and Conrad with her. The remaining knights stood guard. Their escort had swelled in number as they passed through the Knight-Messenger's way stations.

"The Aschenbach," she said, trailing a long stem of grass in the water. "My own little brook. It flows into the great river many miles to the west."

Liese came out of the inn carrying food on a tray. She was excited and started talking before they could hear her.

"Please child, we cannot understand you," said the Countess.

"Those two men, those two nice men from the bandit's hideout," said Liese. "They are here. In the inn. I saw them."

"Do you mean Dachsburg?" asked Conrad. "The ruin up in the rocks?"

"Yes. Dachsburg."

"There were many men while we were there," said the Countess. "I don't recall any who were nice."

"I thought they were nice. Two always together. They knew Flik-Flak. They called me Snow White," said Liese, and she blushed.

Conrad snapped his fingers.

"Dieter and Petrus. Am I right?"

"I think that was their names."

Conrad sprang to his feet.

"My lady, it cannot be a coincidence that they are here, at this time, so close to your castle. They must be here to help Flik-Flak."

The Knights of the Eagle picked up the scent and gathered round.

"Can Flik-Flak himself be far away? Let us seize them."

"Wait, wait. Liese, did they see you? Do they know you recognized them?"

"No. They're in the back, sitting at a table behind the inn. I peeked through the side door. It was only chance I saw them. They were talking and drinking without a care in the world."

"Good. It is my belief that they plan to rendezvous with Flik-Flak, perhaps before the theft is accomplished, perhaps after. I think the wisest plan would be for some of the knights to set a watch on them while the rest of us ride on. That way, if we miss Flik-Flak at the castle, or if we're already too late, perhaps we can catch him when he meets his friends."

"That's a sound plan," said the ranking Eagle Knight. "But we must not set a watch in uniform. You two, cover up!"

It must have been a familiar order and a familiar process. The two designated knights set to stripping, reversing, covering and tucking articles of clothing, crests, emblems and pins until they seemed but two unusually well-dressed travelers. Even their sword hilts they wrapped tightly in black scarves.

The Countess too had arisen.

"We must ride then. Take the food with us."

"If I might be permitted to make one more suggestion, my lady, it would be a mistake to leave in a galloping hurry. We must not let the two bandits suspect they've been identified."

So they sat on the grass and made an unhurried but distracted meal of their excellent provision.

When the time came, they gathered up the remains of the meal, folded up their cloth, packed their utensils, and mounted. They rode out at a stately pace, Conrad and the Countess leading.

They waited until they had left the inn beyond sight and sound. Then Conrad said, "Now, my lady."

They set boots to the horses and hurried away.

"How far, my lady?" called Conrad.

"Fewer than two leagues. It gets hilly."

They rode past trees colored with autumn, over hard-packed path and golden leaves. They passed green fields dotted with cows and vineyards climbing up terraced slopes. As they got closer to the castle, they found the road obstructed in places by large wagons laden with hay, great loads bulging out on either side.

Passing one last vineyard, they entered a wide grassy plain. The Countess pulled up.

"There," she said, pointing with her riding crop.

A lonely green hill rose in the midst of the plain, and on that hill stood Schloss Mittelsbach, as neat a castle as one could ever hope to see. There were a few houses scattered about the foot of the hill, but nothing that could be called a town. The castle stood by itself.

They had slowed their pace to rest the horses, but they quickened again and cantered across the plain, Conrad, the Lady with Liese, and three knights in escort. They passed one last wagon on the road, coming from the direction of the castle, a small covered affair like a gypsy caravan, pulled by a pair of horses. The driver, a fine figure of a woman, was wrapped in long dress and covered by a wide-brimmed hat and scarf. Conrad was briefly but intensely conscious of her eyes on him as the riders passed her on either side.

The entrance of the castle was choked with traffic—it must be some kind of market day, Conrad thought. He passed between tall graceful towers on either side of the gate, but had no leisure to appreciate the cleverness of the castle's construction as he and his horse found a path through the bustle. He worked his way into the courtyard and stopped dead.

He turned his head and looked back through the gate.

The woman in the wagon, the fine-figured woman. She was Peregrina!

THE MAN WAS CALM.

He did not like to be the center of attention, but he was calm because he was sure that he was doing the right thing.

The head of Human Resources explained things to him, while Mr. Noakes looked at the man with curiosity, almost as if he was seeing him for the first time.

"We are officially eliminating your position. You are not being terminated for cause. That way you are eligible for unemployment benefits."

The man thanked him.

"We've been paying into unemployment for years, we might as well get the benefit. It's all on the up-and-up. It's true; we *are* eliminating your position. At your suggestion."

Now that the paperwork was signed and the technical details were ironed out, the head of Human Resources allowed himself to relax.

"This is the first time it's ever happened to me ... that an employee suggested his own excessing."

The man shrugged.

"It seemed inevitable. It is never wise to avoid the inevitable."

"Well, you've been with us a long time," said Mr. Noakes, rising. It was the time for hands to be shaken. "We'll miss you. This is not how I envisioned you leaving. But if it's what you want ..."

When he left the office, the man ran a gauntlet of well-wishers. Charlotte was there and others he barely knew and his particular friends, Kutta and Herrick. He was surprised at the demonstration; he had not thought he was well-liked. He supposed their emotion came from the fear that they might be taking a similar walk soon. Or perhaps, since he was leaving amicably and openly, he was giving them their first chance to bid a decent farewell and they were funneling the frustrated feelings from the previous secret departures into this one event.

He felt suddenly sad that he would not see most of these people ever again. He talked with Kutta and Herrick for some time, while he cleaned out his office and other friends and sympathizers loitered outside.

At length he gathered his scant office belongings into a box and pushed off. He passed the new receptionist–Lydia was off somewhere being trained, having ascended to a new position–walked out the door and left ten years behind him forever.

Only on the drive home did he begin to worry. If, as was likely, he couldn't find another job, and was forced to sell his house and move away from New York, would the dreams continue in a new home? He feared they would not.

THE PEOPLE OF THE CASTLE pressed around the Countess and her horse. Their lady had returned. The Knight-Messengers were trapped with her in the excited throng. Conrad saw no way to get to her. He called out.

"My lady, the treasures. Where are they?"

He felt a great reluctance to tell them about Peregrina. He did not wish to see her arrested. Besides, he told himself, he did not believe that Flik-Flak would make his escape in that way, tucked into a peddler's wagon.

"The treasures?" he asked again.

She heard, and made herself understood half by words and half by signs. There was a round tower off the courtyard and there it was that the legacy of Mittelsbach was kept.

Conrad slid from his horse and hurried through the carts and booths that still littered the courtyard. The tower door was open and he sprinted up the stairs to the second floor, reminded, as he went, of the winding staircase that had first brought him into the Countess of Mittelsbach's presence so long ago.

He threw open the door and found himself in a high-ceilinged room, heavily decorated by hangings and paintings.

There, in the center of the room, stood Flik-Flak, bent over a table. He was endeavoring to free a red banner from a great long flagstaff, without damaging it in any way. He looked up and saw Conrad.

"Too soon, you arrive too soon. Could you not, my friend, have given me another hour?"

"We arranged changes of horse through the Eagle Knights. Even so, we have barely made it in time."

"The knights are here too, then?"

"In the courtyard. With the lady. It was Peregrina who brought you into the castle, was it not?"

For the first time, Flik-Flak showed concern.

"Peregrina. Was she taken?"

"She was not. I have told no one that I recognized her."

"Excellent."

Flik-Flak laid the banner down.

"This is taking too much time. I cannot liberate the cloth and cannot bring such a great long staff from the castle. The ring I could not find. One too big, the other too small. I think however ..."

And he began moving toward the wall, where Conrad now noticed a cream-and-mottled horn hanging, bound at head and foot with gold.

As Flik-Flak moved around the table, Conrad leaped on and over it, drawing his sword as he went. For once, Flik-Flak looked surprised, but even so he stood between Conrad and the horn.

With lowered sword, Conrad showed a thrust at Flik-Flak but when the other stepped back, pulling his own weapon free of its scabbard, Conrad changed targets and slipped his sword under the leather cord that hung the horn on the wall. He raised the tip of his blade and neatly slid the horn down and over the hilt and over his arm, stepping back out of range as he did so.

"Ah. So you contest the possession with me."

"I do."

As they spoke, Conrad quickly took the horn from his sword arm and draped it over his neck and left shoulder, securely behind his back.

"And yet, I notice you do not call for the others. It would be a simple matter to summon aid."

"I suppose it would. But I would not wish to see Flik-Flak taken, no more than Peregrina."

"A good comrade even now," said Flik-Flak. "A man after my own heart, so to speak. If only things were different. But now ..."

It began.

Flik-Flak was famous for his quickness and Conrad felt it immediately. Neither was armored, and Flik-Flak kept his point directed at Conrad, describing triangles and other shapes in the air. Always Conrad was reacting, never pushing his own attacks. He kept backing up, his only recourse to escape Flik-Flak's dancing blade. The tower communicated with the rest of the castle through a wide doorway, and Conrad found himself backing through one room after another, feeling his way around furniture and other obstacles. It was like a nightmare; the rooms seemed to go on forever, like an impossibly long corridor that kept stretching before him.

Already he was punctured twice about the shoulders, only managing on his own account a very light scratch across his opponent's face. He saw stairs behind him and took to them, hoping the uneven terrain would level the playing field for the two unequal opponents. He tried to concentrate on Flik-Flak's legs to throw him off rhythm and scored a light hit, but got a cut across the upper face for his pains. Soon he found himself continually wiping blood away from his eyes with his left hand.

Now they were in the farthest reaches of the castle, past the working areas and servants' quarters, but everyone was still in the courtyard celebrating the return of the Countess. It was in the kitchen at last that Flik-Flak passed his sword through Conrad's right wrist and disarmed him.

Conrad thought for a moment to retrieve his sword with his left hand but Flik-Flak was ready and backed him away. Conrad retreated around the great wooden table in the middle of the room, a sort of island for cutting and preparing food.

"Come, my friend," said Flik-Flak. "You have led me a merry dance, but you must see that it is over. Give me the horn and this need go no further."

Conrad looked over the cleavers and carving knives hanging from racks over the central table. It seemed a desperate expedient with no hope of success. He looked wildly about, and saw against the wall, yawning in another wooden kitchen counter, an opening, the garbage chute, where the cooks and their assistants disposed of the inedible husks, and bones, and spoiled bits not fit for the table.

On a sudden inspiration, he turned back to the island, seized a long heavy knife from its rack and made as it to throw it at Flik-Flak. The other fell back into an *en garde,* and Conrad used the time gained to leap up on the side counter, fit his legs into the hole, and propel himself into the chute.

He slid quickly down the well-slimed track, and landed on a great pile of stinking peels, leafy heads, greasy bones, and mildewed bread, sending one or two resident rats squealing and scurrying. It was dark as a mine, the only light coming from the square hole above, which was soon dimmed by the outline of Flik-Flak's head.

"Well played," he said. "Well played indeed. Undignified but effective. I do not think I will follow you down there, as I don't know if there is a way out. You have defeated Flik-Flak and may keep your prize. I hope we meet one day under better circumstances. *Ade und auf Wiedersehen!"*

And he was gone.

Conrad was racked from half a dozen bleeding wounds, wet with kitchen filth, affronted by a stew of foul smells, and he knew he was stuck where he was until such time as the kitchen staff returned and he could call for help. But he still held the horn.

HE WOULD MISS THESE people, Conrad thought, looking up at his old familiar ceiling in his old familiar room. He would miss them all.

THEY SMELLED IT BEFORE they saw it, a dry tang in the air, a danger.

"Do you smell that?" Conrad asked.

They were returning from dinner, an anniversary of sorts, and Conrad was passing along Diana's block on the off chance that he could find parking.

"Smoke," said Diana.

Already they both feared what awaited them. Conrad slowed and Diana popped her head out of the car and looked up.

"Fire! My house is on fire," she said and was out of the car before Conrad could stop. He jerked the car a few houses down the street and stopped in an open driveway, then ran back to the house.

Smoke was issuing from the topmost window. Diana was forcing her key into the lock with shaking hands.

"The silver!" she said. "My gowns! The piano."

She opened the door and they burst in. The smell was much stronger here than on the street, but as yet there were no flames or smoke visible.

"Do you have a fire extinguisher?" he asked.

"Just this little one."

Conrad seized it and ran up the stairs. Before he could get near the top floor, the smoke drove him back. The heat was frightening. The extinguisher was of no use here.

He ran back down.

"It's too far gone," he said.

Diana was putting down the phone.

"I called the fire department."

"Now. What can we save? Silver first, yes?" said Conrad

"Yes."

"Are the display cases locked?"

"I'll get the keys."

As she unlocked the cases, Conrad carried out their contents and carefully laid each piece next to the stoop, hoping that no one would take the occasion to steal it when he went back inside. By the time he got the third one placed, a fire truck was skirling to a stop. Someone must have pulled the alarm before Conrad and Diana had come onto the scene.

When the firemen entered they cleared Diana and Conrad out. She tried to tell them of her treasures; they were respectful but firm. Some went trooping up the stairs, others clamped the hose to a hydrant while a second truck showed up and began extending a ladder.

They watched from across the street. They had locked the rescued silver in Conrad's trunk, wrapping the pieces up in a big beach towel still Conrad carried with him, though it had been a long time since he had been to the beach. They stood arm in arm and watched the slow ruin of Diana's past.

"Look at it," she said sadly, "My beautiful house. My parents, all my papers and books, all gone."

"I think they'll stop it. I think they got here in time."

"But all that water, pouring through the floor and the walls."

There were many onlookers, but no one spoke to them. Conrad thought most of the neighbors did not even recognize Diana out there on the street.

"It was set," she said.

"Do you think so?"

She looked at him, almost with impatience.

"Don't you?"

"But would anyone do such a thing?"

"It was set. Why would a fire suddenly start? We've never had a fire before. And on the third floor? I have no appliances up there, nothing electrical. It was set."

"If it was, they can find that out. There are arson investigators that can find out how it started."

"They won't find anything. Not for me."

"Why do you think that?"

"Because I am who I am and not who they want me to be. You know it's true."

Conrad dropped the subject, and put his arm around her, and together they watched the long night struggle and the firemen's eventual victory and how they spent almost as much time making sure the fire was dead as they did in killing it.

The firemen would not let them go in to retrieve the rest of the silver, not until the inspectors came in the morning. But they were kind; even after all they had endured in their long battle with the flames, they went in themselves and unlocked four more cases for Diana, and brought the silver out.

Conrad and Diana stood and spoke with the commander while all this was going on. They told him about the trouble they had been having with student protesters and developers, but he already knew. It was natural for fire companies to keep abreast of developments in the community.

"We'll get to the bottom of it," the commander assured Diana.

"What about your other museum pieces, your costumes and such?" Conrad asked.

"Leave them," said Diana. "They're as well where they are. Where would we put them? I'm sure they need to be professionally cleaned anyway. *If* they can be saved."

The commander assured her they would seal the building, then asked, "Is there any place you can stay?"

"You can stay with me," Conrad said. "I have a guest room, my parents' old room."

He gave the commander his contact information. At Diana's request, and following her precise directions, they brought out one more item, a metal strong box containing her important papers. She took the box, thanked them all profusely for their work and their heroism, took one long last look at her wrecked and sodden house, and that was that.

Conrad guided her through the streams of dirty water and foam back to his car, held open the door for her and got her settled. He walked round and took his own seat, and was soon driving along the old familiar road home. Familiar, but this morning it seemed lit with an eerie unfamiliar light.

The way was nearly deserted, and they positively flew over the bridge. They were both as exhausted as if they had been fighting the fire themselves.

"I don't know what I would have done without you," Diana said. "Without you I am quite alone in the world."

CONRAD LOOKED OVER at his clock. He was surprised he had awakened so soon. Diana must still be asleep.

He had put her in his parents' room. The linen was clean, but 'stale' so to speak, and he offered to change it, but she kicked off her shoes and crawled under the covers while he was still talking. Exhausted from sorrow, he thought.

The last thing she said before she fell asleep was, "I'll have to sell now. I don't have the money to rebuild."

He thought of insurance, but knew it wasn't the right time to raise the issue. As she slept, he set out a few comforts, a towel, slippers, a terry cloth robe; such things as he had gathered and kept for the convenience of guests who had never come until that night. Even she had never been to his house before.

Conrad lay in bed in the bright morning and thought, everything has changed. Everything has changed for her and for me. Their lives had taken a turn and neither knew where it would lead. Things go along and go along the same, with the change building under the surface, then the explosion comes and a new life begins. He knew that when the proper time came, very soon, he would ask the woman asleep in the next room to marry him, and he thought that she would say yes. Then they would start a new life together, living somewhere, doing something; a happier life, he was sure. There would be no more dreams.

After these reflections had run their course for an hour or so, he rose and dressed. He put on a pot of coffee, and began cracking eggs. For one or for two? He walked into the living room, under his parents' old bedroom and listened. He heard movement, the old floor creaking again. Breakfast for two.

Just as he finished fluffing the eggs to his satisfaction, Diana shuffled into the kitchen. The terry cloth robe fit her portly figure admirably. Her black hair was unkempt and loose over her shoulders.

"Did you sleep well?" Conrad asked.

She gave a strange, noncommittal shrug and said, "I feel much better."

"Come, sit down."

He poured the coffee, served the eggs and pastry, laid out the butter dish. He sat down across the table from her.

She took a careful sip of black coffee. Then she looked at Conrad with a curious expression in her great wide dark eyes.

"I just had the most extraordinary dream," she said.

About the Author

TERENCE GALLAGHER IS a longtime resident of Queens, NY. He studied Classics at Williams College and Medieval History at the University of Toronto and PIMS, and has a longstanding interest in the culture of old Europe (before everyone got enlightened.) His first novel, *Lowlands*, was published by Livingston Press in 2017, with a sequel, *The Forest Perilous*, slated to appear in 2021. He has also published short stories and poetry in various magazines and journals including *Rosebud, Horla, Two Hawks Quarterly, Candelabrum, Snowy Egret* and *Hrafnhoh*.

Website: https://terencegallagher.wordpress.com

ALSO BY TERENCE GALLAGHER

Lowlands (Livingston Press, 2017)

When James Ward, a high-school freshman living in Queens, meets Cornelia Parsons, he gains entry into a very old, very secretive, and to him very attractive world. Cornelia and her enigmatic guardian Miss Widdershins belong to a confederation of travelers, perpetual exiles who left Ireland and Scotland centuries ago and who now recognize no law but their own. They are facing a crisis brought on by a malignant deserter and Cornelia expects her friend James to take a hand.

https://livingstonpress.uwa.edu/
htm%20(web%20pages)/Lowlands.htm

"A lovely, smart and haunting adventure tale." *Kirkus Reviews*

THE FOREST PERILOUS (Livingston Press, projected publication in 2021)
 A sequel to Lowlands